HERO
COMPLEX

HERO
COMPLEX

TANYA LISLE

SCRAP PAPER ENTERTAINMENT

ISBN-13: 978-1-988911-07-6

www.scrappaperentertainment.com
Email: books@scrappaperentertainment.com

Contents

CHAPTER I

NEW SEMESTER

NO ONE QUESTIONED how the Welcoming Committee had managed to convince the administration to give them their own room, but that was the least of the mysteries that lingered over it. The original founder had vanished in pursuit of the mother that had left their family, which seemed like a death sentence for the committee, but it still persisted. Despite being relatively new to Larkdale Secondary and showing nothing more than a polite interest before this, Indira had swiftly taken over and expedited getting their plan approved.

The room wasn't in the best location, nestled between the electronics and woodworking labs, but the faint hum of saws was comforting to many of the committee members. Their first week was spent improving the sound proofing so that they could talk without yelling while the machines were running. The school had been gracious enough to provide them with any furniture they could desire, making it comfortable enough to provide a welcoming environment, with couches and desks and storage for whatever they could need. By the second, they were showing students around and Indira was coordinating the efforts.

Within a month, they had proved their usefulness. Ten new people had come through, mostly those who had families looking to escape the unpredictability of superhero riddled cities and the dangers that those came with, and they had been able to get each of them settled and caught up within a few days. If they wanted access to clubs that had long since closed their doors to applications, the Welcoming Committee could get them an introduction. If they needed help with their homework or to get caught up with the curriculum, the room was always open and usually had people available to give them a hand. Few people took them up on it, though tutoring wasn't why the room was always occupied.

Indira stopped by, as she did almost every morning. Like others, she was finding it to be a place of solace to get away from the stress of school and everything else that was happening around them. They had pried every speck they could find out of the room and laid sheets of metal over the walls before soundproofing, which made many of them feel safer and less watched inhere, though they still kept their words carefully chosen. It was as safe as any of them could be for now.

She found Shiraz in the corner with Ronnie, taking apart and putting together something that Shiraz was very insistent about not talking about. Her brother had taken to the club more as a reason to keep an eye on her after what happened last semester. She felt bad for scaring him like that, but she thought this was a little much. She was fine now and wasn't inclined to do anything like that ever again if she could help it. That was the whole purpose of the Welcoming Committee.

Laura talked with Matt and Kyle, arms crossed and shaking her head in disapproval. That was always a bad start to the day, Indira knew, and she could feel the conflict coming off of them. Matt and Kyle were supposed to show a new student around to-day, but already Indira could see that it wasn't going to happen as planned.

The good thing was, despite her disappearance at the end of that disastrous mission to look inside the room, Penny was defi-nitely alive. They knew by watching Matt, seeing how slowly he recovered and how pale he looked on any given day because Penny continued to drain him. He still cradled the crutch when he walked after two months, well after the doctors said she should have been off of it. He was weak, but continued to push himself like it was normal. It wasn't so bad some days, but today, Matt looked like he wouldn't even make it through his first class.

"What's happening this time?" Indira asked, slipping in next to Kyle. His hand found hers, their fingers intertwining as he let Indi-ra continue to look between them. She caught Matt's eyes, knowing he would fight her if she tried to tell him to do anything, whether or not he was well enough, but she knew Laura would push the matter.

"He thinks he's showing someone around today," Laura said.

"I am."

"You look like you shouldn't even be in school today." Indira looked back at Kyle, frowning at him disapprovingly. "Why did you even bring him in today?"

"Hey, he looked fine when I picked him up! But they're right, you should probably head home or something."

"I'm fine. Really."

"I was just saying I could go instead of Matt," Laura said, turning to Indira.

Indira turned on her, a curious grin on her face. "You have an exam first period," Indira said. "You don't get to skip those. We already established that. *You* insisted on that stipulation."

"*Brittany* insisted, actually," Laura muttered. "So what, we're sending Kyle on his own? This new girl is our year, so we're running a little low on people we can call on."

"I'll take it," Indira said, turning on Matt. "You can stay here and get a little rest. I'm sure whoever you have first period will get it."

I mean it, she added in his mind. Absently, she rubbed at the back of her right hand. *Penny's drawing on you too much today. You shouldn't go anywhere.*

Matt looked resigned and crossed his arms, shaking his head but accepting his fate. He wasn't happy about this. *You're overextending yourself,* he told her. *Let someone else deal with this.*

Speak for yourself, she said, leading Kyle away to one of the desks. Laura lingered only a little longer before she shook her head and left the room, taking a book out of her purse in the meantime.

She'd been hopeful to miss that exam, Indira could tell, because she hadn't studied. And now she'd wasted her morning trying to get out of it with no luck.

"So tell me about her," Indira said as Kyle brought over the print out that the office provided them about the new student. It was very basic information, just enough for Indira to get an idea of who she was going to talk to. It was a girl named Estelle. She was coming here from across the country from a city that was recently dealing with rebuilding one of their major sectors after a building toppled and her classes...

"That's lucky," Indira said to herself. At Kyle's curiosity she grinned at him before looking back down at sheet again. "Looks like she's got the same schedule as you do. That should make it really easy for her to get caught up."

You knew about this, didn't you? Indira asked Matt.

Let someone else deal with this. They're onto you.

It's probably nothing, but even if it's something, I'm going to have to deal with this sooner than later. I'll bring her here if there's a problem.

Matt wasn't happy with it, but he didn't have any further argument from her as the first bell rang. Matt shook his head before laying back on the couch, closing his eyes and finally giving in to just how tired he was. One of these days, they were going to have to figure out how to cut Penny off from drawing on him, even if that wasn't something Matt was going to want to do. On days like this, she was worried that Matt might not last much longer.

"Raz, class," she told her brother. He kept his head down and she caught the white strands coming out of his ears plugged into his phone. Shaking her head, she smiled apologetically at Kyle before going over into the corner to poke Shiraz hard in the shoulder. He looked up, eyes wide and watering from not having blinked while he was working. He pulled out his headphones and looked at her as she told him again, "Go to class. That was first bell."

"Right, sorry," he said. He quickly wrapped up his project and threw it into one of the cabinets at the back of the room before he rushed out. He took a glance at Indira, a warning to be careful out there, before he left and went off to the test she knew he had first period.

"Shall we?" Indira asked, grabbing her purse and falling in step beside Kyle as they made their way up to the office.

"You're amazing, you know that?" Kyle said, smiling down at her. "I don't know how you keep track of everything like that."

"Raz is always getting stuck in projects like that," Indira said dismissively, knowing full well that he meant much more than just that. "You just have to poke him from time to time to remind him that the rest of the world still exists. No big deal. So long as he doesn't start skipping classes again."

Kyle laughed and shook his head, squeezing her hand a little as they kept walking and opting to let the subject drop for now. Indira let herself listen in on his mind, now buzzing with thoughts of how this must be what it was like to date a superhero. Despite how much time they spent together, he wouldn't be surprised if she went off and fought crime when he wasn't looking in some cat suit. He was very interested in what she would look like in spandex. One of these days, she would have to bring him up to date on what heroes actually wore.

CHAPTER 2

ESTELLE

ESTELLE WAS EASY to spot. She was alone, sitting outside of the front office with the usual package of papers held loosely in her lap. She kept her light brown hair up in a ponytail that she then braided and looked out around at nothing. Her short legs hooked around the legs of the chair, the hem of her jeans threatening to get caught under the heel of her sneakers. As they got closer, Indira could see she had a light dusting of freckles across her nose and pale blue eyes.

Indira knew something was wrong as soon as she saw her. Namely, that she wasn't actually there. She glanced at Kyle, who clearly acknowledged that there was a girl sitting there. Indira looked back at her to find that, while there appeared to be a human girl of about sixteen sitting there, she had no thoughts radiating off of her, nor even the hum of any mental activity. Even those people who blocked off their thoughts had some hum, some sign that they were really there, but there was none of that from Estelle.

It wasn't completely unheard of. Probably. Just because Indira had never run into anyone like her before didn't mean people who were completely immune to psychics were impossible. There were plenty of people out there that were just not affected by certain types of powers and abilities, and Estelle might just be one of those. Chances were that meant that Estelle wasn't even aware of her immunity.

It did mean that Indira couldn't warn her about the place like she normally did and she would have to find another way. If she needed the warning at all. The Welcoming Committee's success so far had been due to their ability to quietly figure out who had powers and warn them about the city and how carefully it watched them. To tell those people that they should get out of town if they could. To tell them not to try to be a hero or a villain here, because they would end up dead all the same, without the blaze of glory or a single soul remembering them.

But people who were immune, they often weren't even aware of their abilities. And the ones Indira had known before had very little desire to get into the business. If Estelle had none of those aspirations, then this would be a normal orientation.

"Are you Estelle?" Kyle asked, taking the lead as Indira lagged behind. He offered s hand and a smile. "I'm Kyle and this is Indira. We're going to show you around today."

Estelle smiled as she stood up, wearing her nerves where Indira didn't need any powers to see. Her eyes shifted between the two of them, taking the hand Kyle offered timidly and letting him give her a single shake before she withdrew it. She blushed and looked down at her hand before she tried to straighten up and look firmly at Indira.

"Hi," Estelle said. She met Indira's eyes and gave Indira a look that she was very well versed with. Indira did indeed see this guy and she was very aware of what he looked like.

Indira tried not to be too endeared. Estelle was still unsettling, but she seemed harmless enough. "Welcome to Larkdale. Come on, we'll show you around."

"Am I going to actually go to class today?" she asked, picking up her backpack and slinging it over her shoulder. "They didn't really tell me."

"The afternoon ones," Indira told her. "But for the morning, think of it like orientation. If you have any questions, let us know and we'll do what we can to answer everything for you. And, I hope you don't mind, but I got a peek at your schedule. It looks like you've got all the same classes as Kyle, so if you need a hand with anything, you can always just ask him."

"Thanks," Estelle said. She looked like she was happy about that, but she wouldn't meet either of their eyes, looking firmly at the ground ahead of them.

The nagging feeling that something was off about Estelle's schedule started to fade and Indira tried to relax. She knew she was relying on her abilities too much, but the practice with them was making her stronger, and she needed to be stronger. At the very least, she needed to be strong enough to keep track of everyone here and keep them all safe.

They started the tour, Indira pointing out how to cut through the school to get to her classes if she ended up late and which teachers she had were going to end up being a problem with keeping people late. They chatted about how far she was at her old school in her classes and Indira was surprised that she seemed to have gotten exactly up to date on the classes that she needed to.

Their tour wound down and Indira still couldn't tell if Estelle was someone she needed to warn about anything or not. She was completely blank, but that might be completely normal for her. Indira didn't know what to do about her but, as Kyle let the conversation dip into his favourite topic, she opted to let it continue. If Estelle was powered in some way, she may let it slip.

"So where are you from exactly?" Kyle asked. "We get people from all over the place. Indira just transferred in last semester from Vancouver."

"Oh, was that because of that guy that was kidnapping all those robotics engineers to build a huge mech suit last year?" Estelle asked, eyes wide and concerned as she looked at Indira. Those blue eyes of hers were almost hypnotizing. "That was all over the news!"

"Yeah," Indira said. "Dad didn't want to get kidnapped again and it was kind of tough on the family."

"Oh my god, I'm so sorry!" Estelle said, pulling herself away as soon as she realized her mistake. For as suspicious as she was, her mannerisms were fairly sweet. "I'm from Dagenham. Some Doctor D guy decided to destroy a bunch of stuff so we ended up here. The one place where it's actually illegal to have superpowers."

"It's not *powers* that are illegal," Kyle corrected her, as he corrected Indira and many others before her. He wasn't irritated at it anymore, only tired. His father was the one that wanted powers suppressed, but he was endlessly fascinated with them. "It's just using them for the vigilante stuff."

"My brother always hated powers and magic and stuff like that. Heroes freaked him out more than villains did because he never knew why they were doing it. I mean, if you had unlimited power, he figured you'd be doing something horrible with them, right? But superpowers look like they'd be so much fun and who wouldn't want to help people, you know?"

Indira let her eyes drift to the walls and she noticed something strange as Estelle talked. Nothing was happening. The walls here were dotted with black specks, always watching and listening, waiting for an opportunity to flash red when someone talked too much about forbidden topics. There were things that Estelle had said there which should have made the specks light up with their red eyes to stare at them, but none of them did. They lingered, still off and not paying her any heed at all. She looked back at Estelle and tried to figure out how she was doing it, but it all sounded straightforward enough to set them off.

"Honestly, this place is pretty dull without them," Kyle said. "I've always kind of hoped that some hero would show up in town and they would bring the whole thing back so that we could actually have heroes and villains and stuff here too, rather than just watching them on television. It's so weird. Like, the rest of the world gets to see these guys with these amazing powers saving the day, and here I don't think there's even anyone *with* powers. At least, no one ever talks about having them."

There they were. They came on when Kyle talked, but shut off soon after Estelle began speaking again.

"Statistically five percent of people have some kind of supernatural ability or some kind of magic, though, right? A lot of it is in families, but not all of it. And there's some people who have really useless ones. And there's some people who pick up stuff that gives them abilities. And there's the heroes that just don't have any powers at all and don a mask and start fighting crime! Hey, if you really want to have heroes here, then maybe—"

"Don't even think about it," Indira said, reaching out for both Kyle and Estelle' shoulders to stop the idea before it got much farther. She didn't need Kyle getting it in his head to start doing that. She didn't need even more people that she needed to keep an eye on. Out of the ten students that had transferred in, six had powers. Out of those, only three were still around and kicking. She didn't need Kyle going that way as well.

As soon as her hand hit Estelle's shoulder, she snapped it back, unable to hide her shocked expression as she stared at her. She might have been solid to touch, but Estelle was *not* there. She was only a projection, the real Estelle hiding somewhere else. Indira had never even heard of anyone who had managed to make a solid projection before this. Something about it felt very wrong. She didn't want to get Matt involved, but she needed a second opinion that wasn't currently in class.

Kyle didn't notice Indira's reaction or the look on Estelle's face, something that might have been confusion or a warning. He took Indira by the hand and leaned in closer to her, resisting the urge to kiss her in front of the new girl. He bumped her shoulder with his own and smiled a smile that made her forgive him for the things he didn't do. "Don't worry, my dad would literally kill me if he caught me doing that. And if I were dead, I wouldn't get to see you anymore."

"Sap," Indira said, shoving him playfully as she looked past him to Estelle. She was definitely a problem that she was going to have to get a second opinion on. A projection should not be solid. "Last stop on the grand tour of Larkdale, since you're getting this so well," Indira said, pushing the idea into Kyle's brain so that he wouldn't argue with her. "There's a study room we have set up so that if you need help just catching up, you can come to us."

"Awesome!" Estelle said, her words coming out in a squeak. If Indira weren't suddenly very suspicious of her again, she'd think Estelle were embarrassed. As it was, she kept her head firm-ly down and eyes averted as they made their way through the school. The pink flush in her face slowly faded away and she said nothing else.

Though the conversation remained impartial and relating mostly to pointing out more rooms and what their purposes were, thoughts of what it would be like to be a real hero continued to buzz through Kyle's mind. He looked to Indira, wondering if she would approve after all the things she had said about heroes so far. Indira would have to make it very clear that she would be against such a thing, especially here.

Kyle stopped at the door, brow furrowed as other thoughts started to enter his mind. "Hey, you think Matt's actually awake?"

"Matt?" Estelle asked, breaking her silence.

"He's also in our year," Kyle said brightly. "And he's in a couple of... *our* classes. If you get stuck with anything, you can always ask him too. He'll be happy to help when he's there."

"When he's there?"

Indira made a quick gesture to tell Kyle to stop talking. "Don't worry about it," Indira said. "Anyway, we use this room for any tutoring if you need to catch up on anything until you're up to date. Not a lot of people take us up on the offer, but it's here if you need it. There's usually someone in here who can help if you need it."

Indira opened the door and was pleased to note that, despite being unconscious, Matt was looking a lot better. He slept on the couch, his crutch laying on the floor beside him, and looked considerably less pale than he had this morning. Unfortunate about the snoring, but she didn't want to wake him. She did need an opinion on Estelle, but she could wait until lunch and ask one of the others to get a look at her.

Shiraz was not doing quite as well. He was working on his device again, now with cords leading out of it and into a computer. His hands were frozen on top of the keyboard, headphones in his ears to block out the sound, his eyes unblinking on the screen. Though his face looked perfectly calm despite not moving, there was a buzz of panic coming off of him that filled the room. That wasn't good.

Shaking her head, she turned back to Estelle. "Excuse me a moment," she said gently. She turned to the corner of the room and went directly for her brother.

Shiraz didn't look up as she approached. Gently, she leaned across the table and pulled the headphones out of his ears, dropping them to the table. She put her hands on his shoulders and gave him a little mental push. It felt like an egg had cracked across her back and the goop was spreading down her arms. She let it continue and forced it over her brother, keeping her voice even as she spoke. "Raz, that was the bell," she told him. "You should probably get some lunch."

"Brother," Kyle offered helpfully to Estelle. Matt continued to snore on the couch as they stood in the doorway awkwardly. Estelle looked back at Indira before she shuffled away from Kyle.

Shiraz's eyes snapped up to her, then over her shoulder before she had fully cut him off from his abilities. She could tell from the look on his face that he had seen something he didn't like behind her, but tried to keep calm. He forced in a few deep breaths and met Indira's eyes again. "What?"

"The bell," Indira repeated. "Lunch time. Remember lunch? Are you feeling okay?"

"Who's that?" Shiraz asked, looking back over Indira's shoulder again.

Estelle looked around and nearly jumped when she realized that Shiraz was looking at her. She offered a wave and continued to look very awkward as she stood at the very edge of the room, looking nearly terrified about coming in any further. Kyle ushered her in and went to kick at Matt's foot to get him up.

"I'm going," Shiraz said, sounding much more worried than his face showed. He unplugged his device and put it back into the cabinet before throwing his laptop back into his backpack. *There's something wrong about her, Indi. She's not there. But she's also... that other thing. Not dead but... I don't know what it is or what* she *is, but it's wrong.*

Shiraz muttered something as he left, looking back to Indira on his way out. He said nothing more, but his look was clear enough. She should be careful of whatever Estelle happened to be. She had never seen her brother shaken like this before.

It confirmed her suspicions that there was something strange about Estelle, but Indira wasn't sure if it was only paranoia on Shiraz's part, or if there was something to actually watch for. If she was one of them, then Indira was going to at least try to keep her from going the same way as so many other students who had come before. Until Estelle did something to prove herself dangerous, she owed her that.

"What?" Matt groaned as he came back to consciousness. He wasn't that happy about being awake to start with, but being kicked awake by Kyle seemed to be another thing altogether. He looked over and saw that he wasn't alone, that another person was there with him, before he snapped himself up on the couch. He doubled over almost immediately after with a groan and grabbed at his still healing side. Matt hissed in a breath as he tried to steady himself.

"Hey, you okay?" Kyle asked. "You didn't have to get up like that. You gotta be more careful."

"Is he okay?" Estelle asked, peeking around from the side of Kyle, her face flushing at the sight of Matt and her eyes averting. Indira was almost sad she couldn't read her mind to see if she had really just developed a crush on Matt after one look at him.

"I'm fine," Matt said automatically, taking a glance up at the pair of them. He would have looked longer, but faked a wince and looked back down again. He took in a deep breath and let his mind loudly spiral as he tried to make sense of what he'd seen.

The hell is she? Matt demanded. *Indira, what the hell is she?*

What are you getting? Indira asked calmly, watching and coming slowly over to join them as Matt tried to straighten himself back up again.

"I'm Estelle," Estelle said in a squeak and she extended her hand. She didn't look up or at him at all, instead carefully studying the ground.

Matt looked back up at her and shook her hand as best he could. "Matt," he said, looking at her carefully. She gripped his hand and looked very happy about it, though she was growing a deeper shade of red with every passing moment. She pulled her hand back and tried to look at him while her nerve held out.

"Kyle and Indira said I was in some of your classes, so I hope you can give me a hand with everything," she managed to get out. "I mean, I'm sure I can probably get it, but just in case I don't get something. I mean, I'll try not to get in your way or anything, but I'll ask if I have any questions? If that's okay."

Matt smiled weakly as she spoke, trying to appear to be nice and courteous and gracious through the pain he was not feeling. He was definitely stronger now than this morning. He rattled off his concerns about Estelle to Indira as she managed to get her words out. *It's like she's not even there,* Matt said. *I don't think she is. But I can touch her even though she isn't there. There's magic on her, but that's not what's doing it. It's like...*

Estelle looked up to Matt, her blue eyes meeting his brown ones. She felt Matt's mind go completely blank in that moment. His eyes stayed forward and he collapsed over to the side on the couch, dropping off of it and landing in a heap on the floor.

Eyes wide, Estelle backed away with her hands covering her mouth as Indira went to Matt's side and started to check to make sure he was breathing. He was still alive in there, she knew, and she rolled him over to check and make sure that he wasn't going to die on her. He looked like he would be fine, but his mind let out only the faintest buzz to let her know that he was still in there.

"He'll be okay," Indira told them. "It's okay. Um, Kyle, maybe you should show Estelle the cafeteria? I'm going to get Matt to a doctor, I think. At least the nurse."

"Okay," Kyle said. Indira encouraged him to relax and feel positive that she had this under control. "You going to join us for lunch?"

Indira nodded. "We all have the same class after, so we'll show you the way," Indira told her, relaxing visibly and waving them both off as they left the room. She needed Kyle gone and she definitely needed Estelle out of there before she started trying to bring Matt back from unconsciousness. First things first, though, she needed to warn the others before they ended up in a similar position.

Magic users of Larkdale, Indira called out to the other four now at the school, hoping they weren't too busy to listen to her. *There's a new girl named Estelle. Kyle's with her now. Laura, you've got fourth period with her. Avoid her at all costs if you can until we know more.*

Why? Laura asked, though she wasn't the only one coming back with confusion.

Call it a safety precaution, Indira said. *Matt's down after just looking at her.*

That seemed to get compliance from them, at least for now. There were only five in the school, and one of them was now unconscious in front of her. She sat more comfortably by his head and put her hand over his eyes, trying to see how far inside his head he'd gone and just where he was right now. Probing deeper, she could hear him still alive in there. Mentally reaching in, she rubbed the back of her right hand as she pulled him out.

CHAPTER 3

GHOSTS

WHILE MATT SEEMED to be doing better lately, the circles under his eyes were getting darker as the days passed. Thoughts concern and fatigue buzzed around him as he started to fall asleep on the textbook as their teacher droned on at the front of the class. Indira nudged his arm to keep him awake and prodded gently at his mind until he let her in.

You okay? Indira asked gently.

Matt shook his head and wiped his eyes with both of his hands. *I'm fine.*

And now you tell me honestly…

Matt shook his head. *It's nothing. Really.*

Don't make me find out for myself.

Try me.

Indira looked at him sidelong and shook her head. She warned him. She felt the walls go up around his mind, but after how much she'd been using her own abilities lately, it posed no problem. She didn't want to pry too deeply, only concerned with what was making him look so worn. She knew nightmares couldn't be keeping him up. Magic users didn't dream or have nightmares. He seemed to be able to fall asleep just fine, so something else had to be happening.

She found the culprit almost immediately. He'd been seeing Penny in his sleep. She was fading away at times, while other times she was desperately trying to fight back. She was in pain and desperately trying to break free when her mind was together. She didn't know what was happening to her, but she kept calling for Matt, hoping that he would come back for her, and it was eating him up that he wasn't doing anything.

The pang of guilt was something Indira was quick to shove away as she pulled back. The back of her hand was red and itched painfully, and she pressed it into the cool of the table. She wasn't sure how he was seeing what was happening to Penny, but it made sense that Matt wasn't sleeping if he was seeing that. She wasn't sure she would be able to handle the guilt of leaving Penny behind if she was seeing her like that every night.

Not that they were going to leave her there, but Matt was going to burn out before Indira could figure out how to get her out of there at this rate.

You could have just said it was Penny, Indira told him as their English teacher wrapped up the lecture portion of the class for the day. The class discussion topic turned to the upcoming group presentations, Indira paying very little attention. *You know you can tell me if this stuff is happening.*

It's not a big deal, he said. He stifled a yawn next to her. *Besides, you're the one who wanted to stay out-*

You can't make me stay out of it, Indira snapped back at him. She rubbed again at the back of her hand. *I can handle a little itching. Look, I can't stop you from getting yourself caught like her, but I can try to help you get her out of there. I don't want to leave her behind either. You're not the only one with someone in there, Matt.*

Yeah? And who do you have?

Indira resisted the urge to roll her eyes. *Quantum*, she reminded him. *The guy who got himself caught trying to save you guys on Halloween. And Penny. I'm not exactly blameless in getting her caught.*

Matt's sidelong gaze was skeptical. *I don't... that hero guy? There was a hero there that night, wasn't there? How did I forget about that?*

You don't remember Esther half the time either.

"Hey," Kyle said, both of them turning to see him at their table with Estelle in tow. He smiled brightly at Indira. "You guys want to do this together?"

Indira smiled and said nothing, looking back to Matt. He hadn't exactly had a good reaction to Estelle before and, though he could be in the same room with her, he hadn't talked to her since that day. He was careful not to be too close, excusing himself to the Welcoming Committee room for lunch so he could take a nap instead of joining them.

Estelle had been avoiding him as well, though her actions were usually coupled with a blush, sudden lack of eye contact, and some hurried reason why she shouldn't linger for too long. Now, she stood firmly behind Kyle, looking like she was determined to be normal around Matt this time.

"Sure," Matt said. He didn't feel happy about it, but his face showed none of that. "So who was actually paying attention?"

They settled into discussing the project, Indira surprised to find just how much Estelle was picking up and how well she seemed to work with Kyle and Matt. The three of them took care of a lot of the details of the project while Indira offered a helpful note or two, but by the time the bell rang, they had already split up the assignment and Indira wouldn't be surprised if they actually managed to get this done by the end of the week, despite how Matt kept looking like he was going to collapse into his textbook.

As they got their stuff together at the end of class, Indira reached over and put her hand on Matt's shoulder, ignoring the burning sensation that flared across the back of it and letting the goopy feeling trail down her arms and forcing it over him. He froze and looked back at her sharply, trying to pull away, but she didn't let him go until she could feel it finally cut him off from his magic, if only for a little while.

"Maybe you should get some sleep," she suggested. It's temporary. You look like you're going to fall over. Just try to get some rest.

Matt pulled himself out from under her hand, shaking his head at her. He muttered an apology to Kyle for skipping lunch with them again and left without another word, hobbling away on the crutch. Indira was fairly certain he was too tired to do anything rash and hoped that he would actually take the chance to grab a nap. Part of her considered cutting him off like this more often, just so that Penny would stop draining on him and he could heal enough to get off that crutch at last.

"He should really be off that thing by now," Kyle muttered as he slipped his hand into Indira's.

"Is he going to be okay?" Estelle asked as she fell in step beside them and they headed for the cafeteria. "He still looks kinda sick."

"He says he'll be fine," Indira said. She wished Estelle could have found somewhere else to be for lunch, but she hadn't made any other friends in her classes besides Indira and Kyle. It wasn't exactly a bad thing, Indira able to keep a better eye on her, but she was finding herself wishing for a break from her now and then. Kyle didn't seem to notice.

"He'll be okay," Kyle assured her. "He's had a lot to deal with, right? It's good that he's got people like Indira keeping an eye out for him. So long as you're not *too* there for him..."

Indira laughed and bumped her hip into his. "Not a chance," she said. "Although, I didn't get a chance to see who that new guy Brittany was supposed to be showing around today. She did mention something about him being very tall, dark, and mysterious..."

"He isn't," Kyle said a little too quickly. She could already tell where his thoughts were going, that he sounded just like the sort of guy that might be a hero by night. Part of him was almost willing to let Indira dump him for this new guy if that meant that they could have heroes in Whitten.

"Jealous?" Indira asked, bumping into him again with a coy smile. There was something about the new guy's name that seemed almost familiar, but she didn't know why. "I haven't even met the guy. But with a name like Damien Blackwood, don't you think he just kind of deserves to have some sort of alternate identity, patrolling the night, giving your dad a headache?"

The smile on her face faltered as she realized what she was saying. What was she doing?

"Don't get my hopes up."

"Whitten can't just *not* have a hero forever, though," Estelle chimed in. "Eventually, someone's gotta show up and start trying to help out, right? It's not like your dad can actually get rid of every superhero in existence or keep any of them from coming here. Eventually, someone's going to show up to help with the crime that actually does happen here."

"He's going to try," Kyle said, still bitter and doing nothing to hide it. "He's worked pretty damn hard to make sure there's none here now. It's, like, his life's mission to make sure they don't ever get in the way of his work ever again or something."

Indira tapped at her pocket. She could have sworn she felt her phone vibrate, but it must have been her imagination.

"But people become heroes all the time, right?" Estelle pressed. They grabbed a table for lunch, Estelle leaning in as her eyes grew wide and hands more animated. "I mean, all it takes is one lab accident, right? And it's not like we don't have a bunch of labs and bio-engineering places and robotics labs in Whitten. So if something happens in one of those, someone might become a Whitten born hero. And if he's local, then maybe it's okay?"

"I think you're underestimating my dad's hatred for anything and anyone who tries to get in the way of police work," Kyle said, laughing now through the bitterness. He never liked what his father had done, but there was little he could do for the moment and he knew that. Though, now Indira could feel more ideas growing in his head. Dangerous ones.

"What if it were family, though?" Estelle asked. "He couldn't get mad at *family*, right?"

"You are really into this idea that Kyle become a superhero," Indira said. "Which, in Whitten, is pretty damn illegal." Indira wondered if this was her angle the whole time. To find some way to convince Kyle to become a hero and take on his father. Indira could see him eventually doing it with enough prodding, but she wasn't going to be happy at all if that's what it came to. He would just be a guy in a suit and she was pretty sure he would go down like a brick in the river as soon as he realized what all the powered people in town were actually dealing with. If he ever found out about the powered people in town.

"She just doesn't want me in spandex," Kyle said, grinning at her. "At least someone thinks I'd do good in it. But even if I did, it's not like there's anyone to really fight, right? I mean, we have police and they deal with all the normal crime. If you're going to have a superhero, you need super crime to fight against. And I don't really want someone to go around starting to knock over buildings or kidnap people."

"So if there *was* something happening…"

"My boyfriend is not going to become a superhero," Indira said firmly, reinforcing the thought in Kyle's mind. She could feel him waver and consider the idea. She could tell that Estelle was doing something to push her own ideas into his head, but she was quick to push them back out again. He didn't need any more encouragement. "Not if he wants me to stick around, anyway."

"You heard the boss," Kyle said, perfectly happy about this arrangement. Kyle was more interested in idolizing heroes than becoming one himself. He would be content dating a hero and he liked to imagine that he was doing just that with Indira, even if she was fairly vocal about how much she would rather never become one herself. In quiet moments, he liked to think that was just part of her cover.

"So how are you doing here," Kyle said instead, letting the subject change as the battle over who got the final say over which ideas got pushed into his mind came to an end. "Adjusting okay? I know it's probably a lot different from school back wherever you're from."

Again, Indira felt something in her pocket. Her phone was doing something strange and she ignored it.

Estelle shrugged. "I'm catching up in the classwork fine," she said. "I've just never been that good at meeting people, you know?

I'm really glad you guys keep putting up with me. I'm sure you weren't expecting to have to deal with me for this long."

"Hey, it's what we're here for," Kyle said. "If you need help with anything, you can just ask."

"Well, there's maybe one thing," Estelle said, getting very quiet and looking carefully around. Her eyes didn't quite meet either of theirs as she tried to put together the words. "It's okay, though. It's stupid."

"No, really," Kyle insisted. "Anything."

"You don't want to promise that," Brittany said, coming up from behind them and making all three of them jump as she set her hands down on the back of Indira's chair. Indira snapped around to look at her, trying to figure out when she got there and how she'd managed to sneak up on her. Normally Indira could tell when someone was coming from a way off. Brittany smiled apologetically at Estelle and Kyle. "Sorry, need to borrow Indira for a bit. You mind?"

"Go ahead," Kyle said.

"See you after school?" Indira asked.

"I've got practice. Dinner tomorrow, though, right?"

Indira nodded and got her things together. "Tomorrow night," she said, smiling.

"Just ignoring your phone?" Brittany asked quietly as she led Indira away.

"What?" Indira pulled her phone out of her pocket, finding that she had missed twelve messages in the last hour, all from Brittany.

That was strange. She checked her settings and saw that it should have been vibrating when she received them. Brittany was making no secret of why she thought Indira had been ignoring her and, glancing back to see Estelle leaning across the table to keep talking to Kyle, she was inclined to consider the possibility.

CHAPTER 4

OUTSIDE INFLUENCES

BRITTANY HANDED HER a granola bar and shook her head as they walked. "I swear, you are going to get yourself killed with the company you keep," she said. She was irritated, but glad when Indira took the granola bar without protest. "Really, Indira, you don't get to make yourself the centerpiece of this and then take lunch with the enemy."

Indira's eyes flickered around, catching a flash of red. Brittany caught it too, but she was too annoyed to care. "What are you talking about?" Indira asked. She was starving and ripped into the granola bar, covering her mouth as she took too large of a first bite. Around her, she could start to hear the sounds of the ambient minds around her again, filling the silence that she hadn't noticed before.

"Do you normally not eat anything during lunch?" Brittany asked her instead. "Or is that a new thing since you started hanging out with that thing?"

Indira blinked. Neither she nor Kyle had actually gotten any food before sitting down with Estelle. It was a strange thing to not notice but, now that she thought about it, she hadn't gotten food any of the times that Estelle had joined them for lunch. All week, she had gone back to class so hungry, but she had assumed she just needed a snack.

"I don't like that new girl," Brittany said when they rounded the corner. "I want to know what she's after. She's spending too much time with you."

"She's in all of Kyle's classes," Indira told her. "And I'm not going to stop going out with him just because you think it's a bad idea."

"You're drawing too much attention to yourself," Brittany told her. "But that's not why I need you right now. Damien needed something and I wanted to see if you could talk to him and give him a hand with it. He seems to think he might know you. And after, we need to have a word."

Indira looked sidelong at her and nodded. She knew what that meant and she was ready for it. It was why she had kept up with the Welcoming Committee after all. This right here. Helping them make sure nothing happened to anyone else. That was what it was all about. Although, she wasn't sure about the second part of that statement. "What's his name again?" she asked.

"Damien Blackwood."

"And you say *I'm* drawing too much attention to myself." Still, she frowned. That name sounded familiar, but she couldn't place why.

"He's pretty sure he knows you," Brittany said again. "Transferred in from Vancouver High. Your old school, right?"

"We'll find out soon enough." Her stomach rumbled.

Did you want to have that word now? Indira asked. *Can it be quick? I think I need to go find something to eat before class.*

We're not going to just keep sitting around waiting for the next person to kick it, Brittany told her. *We can't just keep waiting and hoping that nothing happens. Matt's fading after whatever the hell happened in the winter. You still haven't told anyone what that was. And we want to know. We don't want to keep hiding like this. It's suffocating.*

Indira nodded. *I know,* she said. It wasn't like she didn't see it coming. *You were right, though. It's to keep everyone safe. We can't take this down. There have been stronger people who've tried. Everyone who tries ends up going down and we can't just keep throwing people at this problem and hope that we come out on top.*

I can't just keep watching him wither away like that. Brittany shook her head. *And I can't just keep not doing anything while we get picked off.* She was older and she was going to get out of here soon, but Laura was going to remain here for another year and she was hesitant to leave without her. They all knew it wasn't safe for them here. And so many of them had a desire to fix things, to do more than just survive. They all wanted so badly to make it out of there and save as many people as they could in the process. Even those that didn't have a heroic streak.

And who has gotten picked off? Indira asked.

Brittany rounded on her in the empty hall, incredulous as her mouth opened. The anger in her eyes faded as she said nothing, calming into confusion. She was so sure there were people. She *knew* there were people. Why couldn't she remember them.

Jane? Indira offered. *Jane Riker. She thought she could save people and she ended up getting herself killed. You liked her, you said. Thought she had spunk. And now you can't even remember her.*

We aren't just sitting around and waiting, Brittany told her. *You are telling us what happened that night and you are going to tell us what happened with Matt.*

Indira walked past her, tugging her along by the shoulder until she followed on her own. *Just Matt?* she asked. *I think you're missing a few people in there. Or have you forgotten what else changed over the winter break. Penny. Remember her? If you try, you'll kind of remember someone told you that she ran off, but you can't remember who. And Esther. Do you even remember Esther? She's got a grave now. There's a reason I haven't wanted to do this.*

Brittany looked stricken, but she kept walking. She didn't remember the names at all until Indira mentioned them and, now that they were back, she didn't know what to do about them. Her desire to do something about all of this wavered as she started to realize that she wasn't going to even be remembered if she was lost. If Laura was lost in all this, she might not remember her until someone said her name. And who would say her name again if Indira got herself killed from being too careful? Who was going to remember any of them?

I'll still do it, Indira told her. *No problem. But you're all going to have to know what you're getting into. This isn't like anywhere outside of Whitten. You're better off grabbing Laura and making a run for it, not staying here and fighting. It's going to get you killed, staying here.*

And not you? I get that you're more powerful than your average psychic if you could cheat the test, but I don't see you leaving. Instead you keep hanging out with I don't even know what she is.

"Oh." Indira stopped walking at that, a realization hitting her. Indira had cheated the test, yes, though more because she was clever than powerful. She had wanted to because she was terrified of the rumours of recruitment and that she might be forced into becoming a hero if they knew what she could do. But Estelle was powerful and she had a heroic streak to her. She wouldn't have tried so hard to hide what she could do. And if they knew what she could do...

"Oh?" Brittany asked out loud, her voice accusing as she stopped next to Indira. "Oh what?"

She had been fighting Estelle earlier, pushing thoughts in and out of Kyle's mind. Normally, that particular ability was caught early and restricted immediately, only unlocked under specific circumstances. Part of the powers test was to find abilities that kids shouldn't have and lock them away until they were properly trained, if the powers could be trained in a responsible manner at all. They would have caught that ability in her and locked it away immediately.

"She's not locked," Indira said, concerned. "How is she not locked?"

"The hell are you talking about?" Brittany asked as they got closer to the room.

"Not your problem," Indira told her, pushing the thought into the corner of her mind and out of the way for now. "You wanted to call it today?"

"You don't get to just—"

"Today it is," Indira said, a final note in her voice. "And I will deal with everything else until then. You don't worry about the rest of it. If you want to get everyone together to find out how to get yourselves killed, who am I to stand in your way? Just remember, *I* didn't ask for this."

"Don't act like you don't want to do it as much as I do," Brittany said.

"You didn't like it when Penny did it."

"Penny isn't here anymore," Brittany snapped. She was clinging to the name and the memory as much as she could, though it was already slipping away from her again. "And she at least wanted to do something. Doing nothing and hoping for survival isn't going to work anymore. I just didn't like her making me feel like I had to do it. Now that we're doing nothing, I'm going nuts."

Besides, I haven't gotten a chance to test out these new powers yet, Brittany told her. *You never realize how much you miss using your powers until you get new ones you don't get to try out.*

You're going to get yourself killed with that attitude.

Indira shook her head and reached out to everyone in Larkdale Secondary who might have something to add to this. *Meeting after school in the club room.*

She got some chatter back, mostly surprised and confused that anyone was contacting them at all, but there was a general feeling of understanding that came back at her. She looked at Brittany and let out a breath. "So, Damien Blackwood?"

Brittany went in first, Indira following after to see the back of someone sitting across from Scott, Brittany's partner for the tour, as he was helping him go through what materials he'd missed so far in the semester. Matt was vacant from the couch for once and her brother was actually in class, giving Indira a chance to focus on why that back made her very worried.

"Damien, this is Indira. She's in charge of the program. If you need anything special, she's the one you call. Indira, this is Damien."

"Indira Mehta," he said, amusement in his voice as he slowly turned around. "You know, your friends back home are really pissed at—"

"Go home, Damien," Indira said. She knew him as soon as he sat up. Before he'd fully straightened up to his full six foot height. Before she saw the strong nose or the pale skin or striking green eyes. "He's not here. You shouldn't be either."

"What the fuck, Indira?" Brittany demanded.

Scott shifted uncomfortably at the table. His eyes found Brittany's. "Should we go?"

"Nah, this is going to be interesting," Brittany said. She swept around to the couch, dropping down and watching Indira with arms crossed and looking displeased. "I don't think I've ever seen her *this* pissed off, and I've seen who she's taking lunch with."

Damien got to his feet, towering over Indira, though she didn't flinch. He remained amused, watching her with a grin and a dare dancing in his eyes. "And who says I'm here for someone? Maybe I'm here to get a first class education in a school free from the distractions of heroes constantly destroying the city and kidnapping the students. Maybe I'm here to tell you that your friends back home are pissed that you stopped calling a week after you moved here. Maybe I'm here to—"

Quantum is dead, Damien, Indira told him, not breaking eye contact as she watched his face freeze and falter. *You need to get out of here before you are too.*

It took a moment for the shock to wear off, Damien breaking it with an awkward laugh. "I always knew you could do something."

"You don't have parents keeping you here. You can go. It's not safe."

"Life's not—"

"*I swear to god,*" Brittany said loudly from the couch. "Finish that and *I'll* send you somewhere so far away you'll never get back."

Scott had settled into the opposite end of it, as far away from Indira and Damien as he could. Indira was blocking the door and he didn't want to get in the middle of whatever this was. Already, he was fading away from sight. Brittany followed Indira's eye and smacked him, bringing him back to full visibility.

"Look, even if I believed he was dead, which he's *not*, I can't go yet," Damien told her. "A whole bunch of people keep coming here and—"

Stop talking, Indira said, closing the distance between them and clamping her hand over his mouth. *First rule of Whitten. You do not talk about heroes, villains, powers, or anything related to those things. You do and you will get yourself killed. You got me?*

Damien looked at her. He was skeptical, but he still nodded. *There's a few people in town. We're all looking for people who've gone missing. Is Quantum really dead?*

Indira let him go. She let out a breath and put a smile on her face to replace the scowl that had been etching itself deeper into her features. "If you're not going anywhere, then welcome to Larkdale High," she said. "If you were at all interested in the Welcoming Committee, a few of us are going to be getting together after school."

CHAPTER 5

STANDSTILL

INDIRA THOUGHT SHE'D gotten out early enough to be the first one there, but the sound of chatter and a squeaking ladder in the dark let her know otherwise. She could see her brother standing on top of it, screwing something into the ceiling next to the light, and Ronnie underneath him holding the ladder in place. She didn't come in, waiting by the light and trying not to raise her voice enough to scare him off the ladder. "The hell are you doing?" she snapped at the pair of them.

"I finished the thing," Shiraz said, screwing in the last bit and knocking it to make sure it was on. "Can you flip the switch?"

Indira turned it on, light filling the room and illuminating the device now fastened to the ceiling. There was no way the school would allow this if they found out, though Indira was more curious about just what it was. There was a faint hum echoing through the soundproofed room that hadn't been there before. Shiraz's machine was a flat mess of circuits that had only a cursory panel screwed over top of it to keep from spilling over, the wires barely hidden beneath it.

"What is that?"

Shiraz ignored her and sat down on top of the ladder. He reached into his pocket and pulled several small black orbs, specks that they'd worked so hard to get out of the room.

"Raz what the hell are you doing with those?"

Shiraz held up a hand for her to be quiet and paid no attention to the door opening again. Matt and Laura appeared in the door and stopped next to Indira, following her eye to watch what he was doing. They didn't catch what was in his hands at first, but they were very alert at the words that came out of his mouth.

"Superhero," he started. "Superpowers. Villain. Telepathic. Telekinetic. I can hear things sometimes."

"Raz, shut up!"

"It's working, though," he said, showing her the specks and the fact that they were not reacting at all. "Ronnie just took these from the hall. They're working. But now they can't hear us thanks to this thing," Shiraz said, proudly tapping on the device in the ceiling. He grinned and looked down at them, tossing them the orbs. Laura jumped away from them while Indira reached out to snatch them from the air. "Won't work far," Shiraz continued. "The range is only about ten metres. We can still probably trigger the ones at the edge of the range if we're too loud but, with the sound proofing we did, we should be okay in here, at least."

"You have got to be kidding me," Indira said. She chucked the specks into the bin by the door and stormed over to him, her mind spinning with so many things she wanted to tell him that they were getting mixed up in there. "This— *This*— All this time you've been—"

"It's okay," he said quietly as he came down from the ladder. "I'm making a bigger one for the house now that I know this one's working. Just gotta make sure it stays working. It should be good, though."

"Do you even know how *dangerous* this was, Raz?" she demanded of him as more people started to filter in. "If you had said just one thing wrong…"

"Like I wouldn't have seen it coming," he said. "Me, of all people. Come on, Indi."

Indira let out a breath and Ronnie put the ladder to the side of the room, sitting with Raz in the usual corner as Shiraz opened up his computer and started working again, though now that this thing was installed she dreaded what his next project was. She didn't have time to worry about what other dangerous thing he was getting into right now, though. More people came in and started to settle around the room.

Sixteen of the twenty two students Indira had sent word out to showed up to the call. She knew it was short notice, that some had no interest in revealing themselves, or had other plans after school. Still, Indira was surprised. The brevity of the message, apparently, had been the motivating factor. Those here were wondering what this was about and hoping that there was a plan underway so that they could stop living like this.

Brittany was at her side as soon as she was certain everyone was there while Laura closed the door behind them and leaned against it to keep anyone else from sneaking in. They looked nervous, some of them seeing one another for the first time. Many of them weren't even aware that there were this many others and they weren't sure if they were exposing themselves by showing up, but they had all trusted Indira so far.

"Whenever you're ready," Brittany told her, suddenly looking uneasy and unsure of things. "Um, when we used to do this—"

"It doesn't matter how it used to go," Indira told her, not meeting her eyes as she looked around. It felt like they were painting a target on themselves and Indira wasn't okay with putting this many people at risk. She wasn't even sure if it was a good idea to do this in the first place. She didn't know what Brittany might do with whatever information she was going to try to force out of Indira, but she could already sense that she wanted to try to make another run at whatever they had found last semester.

Indira could tell already that this meeting was a bad idea, but it was too late to stop it now. At the very least, she was going to make sure that the only people agreeing to whatever plan came out of this were ones who were going to actually survive. She looked over to Shiraz, who seemed know what she was thinking, and nodded. He also placed a couple more specks from his pocket on the desk next to him to keep an eye on, ready to stop her if they flared back up again.

"I'm sure you're all wondering why you've been called here," Indira said loudly to the room, getting them to settle down enough that they were paying attention to her. "First and foremost, if you'll look up, we have a new addition to the room that I thought I should mention before I freak anyone out. We can speak freely in here so long as we aren't too loud about it. So for those of you who are still wondering and now sure about it, let's be clear. Everyone in this room has some kind of superpower or magic. Say hello."

The rumble that went through the room at the sheer discomfort of what Indira had just said was palpable. Those who had been there for years looked immediately to the walls and ceilings, now covered by a layer of soundproofing, looking for the specks that were now covered by the foam. The rest were just nervous, all of them knowing that they were likely being listened to because they were told so, though they didn't know what exactly triggered the specks to listen yet.

"It's been brought to my attention that some of you would like to not have to be scared of saying things like that," Indira continued. "As some of you are already aware, since the new year started, only three of the new transfers in have died. This is, I've been told, a bit of a record. Personally, I'd like to keep everyone from dying, but that's not enough. Some of you want to be able to speak freely and do as you want without having to convince your families to move out of this town."

"Wait, *how* many people have died?" Ronnie asked, surprised that anyone was gone at all. It was a sentiment echoed by the others.

"Three," Indira told him. "The purpose of the Welcoming Committee has been to warn everyone who comes in that you're going to be watched and monitored and, if you don't keep the fact that you have abilities under wraps, you are probably going to get killed for them because you've said the wrong thing. The part I've neglected to make clear is that once you're gone, it becomes a lot more difficult for most people to even know that anyone is missing. You're sad for a bit, then you forget. For those of you who were here last year, you might remember that Penny was the originator of this whole project."

Indira looked out around the room, many of them looking like they knew the name. Some remembered the girl who was rumoured to have run off to find the mother who left town without a word. Others looked at Matt, remembering that he was her brother, and wondering if that was why he was still on a crutch. When she died, had she taken some of him with her?

"Penny isn't the one who died," Indira said quickly. "But she is gone, and we don't have a way to get her back. We haven't made any attempts to take down or dismantle the people who have put these things in place to keep us quiet because doing so right now is what I would consider a suicide mission. But there are those among us here who would rather that we actually do something about that."

Brittany took that as her cue. "And that's where I come in," she said, though she took a cursory glance around the room at anything that might be flashing before she continued. "Now, it's not going to be safe. It's dangerous and we don't want anyone else to lose their lives doing this, so…"

"Who died?" This time it was Alan who asked, looking distressed as he tried to remember another face. Nothing was coming to him.

"Esther," Indira said. Her voice wasn't loud, but it seemed to echo throughout the room. Many of them knew the name from last semester and the fact that she had gone without anyone even remembering her made an impact. She could feel the room go dead, hesitation rising in those who could recall her. "There was a funeral. Some of you were even there."

"We understand if you don't want to do this," Brittany said, pressing onward. "There's a lot of stuff to lose if it doesn't work. And if we're going to make it work, we need to make sure everyone wants in on it. If you're okay with not helping in this, you can leave now. From here on out, it's only going to get worse. If you're not interested, you don't need to be here to hear what the rest of us are doing. I guarantee you that you'll stay safe if you just keep doing like you've been doing."

Several people wanted to leave. Indira looked around the room and gave them the extra push to actually get up and gather their stuff. Damien lingered, curious, though every other person who had only arrived since the start of the semester left. Others, bothered by how little they remembered those who hadn't made it, followed.

Indira looked to Shiraz, who wasn't even paying attention as he kept to his project, his fingers clicking quietly in the background and occasionally looking at the specks beside him. Brittany glanced over at him as well, more because she still wasn't sure why he was here, but ignored him. She wondered what he could even do and assumed it was something technical with the way he was working.

Once the door closed behind them, Brittany turned back to Indira. "Now that that's done, I think we all want to know what happened back in the winter. Because we all know something had to have happened back then. We lost two people and Matt's, well…"

"Matt nothing. You only just remembered that you lost two people now," Indira reminded her. "And that's the *second* time I've told you about them today." She shook her head and looked at Matt before she pushed herself off of the wall and uncrossed her arms. She took a seat on a desk and let out a breath.

"Most of you are aware that something happened," Indira said, peering around the room and seeing how many people were paying attention and trying to remember what little they'd heard. Even Shiraz was paying attention, lowering his headphones, though his fingers didn't stop. Come to think of it, she hadn't even told him what happened. She felt guilty for not saying something to him before, but he had been treating her like she was made of glass since then.

"Someone I know got taken by Whitten. A hero named Quantum. And when he did, I found out where he was being kept. Penny and Matt have someone in there that they were looking for as well and Penny wanted to go in and get them out. Esther was there as well because, well, most of you knew Esther." Indira took a breath to steady herself. It was hard to talk about, but if she went quickly, she could make it. "It didn't end up that well. Esther died saving Penny and Penny got me and Matt out of there, but she's still in there somewhere. She's alive, but if we went back now, we'd probably get ourselves killed."

Shaking her head, Indira let her eyes come back into focus and she looked around at the room, finding that she still held their attention. They were a mix of shocked and depressed at the news, but they didn't know what else to make of it.

"You said Quantum was dead."

Indira met Damien's eyes and scowled. "You can still get out of here, Damien. Just go home."

"There's no way that's everything," Brittany said. "What actually happened in there? And where is this place? Under one of the towers?"

Indira shook her head. "I'm not telling you where it is unless you've got a plan," Indira told her. "We've already lost too many people and I'm not risking any more going down because someone was impulsive and thought they knew what they were doing. I already made that mistake once and I don't want to deal with any more losses. Going after them right now is a bad idea until we learn more."

"So what else happened down there?" Brittany pushed. "We all know you're holding out on us."

"I didn't look into the place enough," Indira said finally. It was best to take responsibility for it now and not wait for them to find out how badly she screwed it up at a later point. "I was projecting in and I only saw the one hall with the guards going up and down it. There was a back entrance and it looked good until they got down there and found the full labyrinth. There were a lot more people watching the halls than I thought. And the place where they're keeping people, it does something to you when you get too close. I couldn't get close enough to see. They were just supposed to find out what was there, but in the end…" Indira shook her head. "It wasn't worth it. Go in to save two people and we lost two people instead. It's not worth it, Brittany."

"You're leaving something out," Brittany said. No one else said a word, watching silently and not wanting to interrupt the delicate dance and battle of wills happening. Indira looked more and more broken with each passing moment, and Brittany looked more and more determined. "If someone actually got the chance to go in there, we could map the place out. We could come up with a plan. We could do *something*. There has to be a way to take all of this down. We don't have to just sit here and hope everything turns out okay."

Scott, Cheryl, Noa, Shiraz warned her. *They aren't lasting long if they stick around.*

"Scott, Cheryl, Noa," Indira said, looking up and pointing each of them. "Leave."

"What, why?" Noa demanded. "I was a hero back home, dammit! I used to save people, not just sit around and hide all the time! Do you know how hard it is to just sit around and do nothing when I *know* that there's people out there that I could be helping? Who are you to tell me that I can't help people!"

"If she wants to be here, then she should be here," Brittany said. "We can't just tell people who want to do this that they can't."

"Because if you stay, you're going to die," Indira said coldly, meeting Noa's eyes as she said the words. She felt so tired. "All three of you are. And I am not going to have anyone else die because of me. So you leave and you leave the rest of this to us. We'll call you if there's a way for you to help without losing your lives."

Like most people, they didn't really think that they were actually going to die doing any of this. Noa wanted to call her bluff, but she couldn't tell if it was really something Indira was capable of seeing. None of them were. Indira had already pulled out enough tricks that they weren't quite ready to take that chance.

"We can't do nothing forever," Noa told her. Indira caught a good look at her manicure as she flipped her off on her way out.

Thankfully, the other two went on their own after her. As the door closed behind them, Laura put her hand on Matt's and squeezed it tightly in support. Indira didn't have the energy to stop her and her ulterior motive. Brittany turned her attention to his corner of the room as well and raised an eyebrow as Laura nodded.

"Matt was there too, right?" Brittany asked. "So Matt, what's really got Indira so worried about going back? It can't just be what happened."

"Iris," Matt said, though he looked like he was in a trance as he said it. "She said there was something else in there with us that pulled her in and trapped her there."

"It was always there whenever I went down," Indira cut in, knowing where this was going. Laura relaxed her grip on Matt and Indira pushed the idea that Laura should stop that into her as she kept talking. "I was never sure what it was, but she was always there. She got me stuck once, but I figured that was because I got too close to that room. I didn't think she could actually pull me completely out of my body and in there completely like that. If not for Penny, I would have never gotten out of there at all. And I almost didn't make it back afterwards."

Brittany looked her over. She was still skeptical, but she turned back to Laura. Laura looked startled and tried to reach out for Matt again. "And where is this place."

"No, Brittany," Indira said. "If you go there, you aren't going to make it back. I don't care how prepared you think you are, I don't care if you think you're going so you can have a look to *become* more prepared. You aren't going to make it out of there."

"Because you can see that," Brittany almost spat at her. "I'm sitting here trying not to get my ass killed for saying the wrong thing every day, but I guess I should just be coming to you every morning to find out if today's finally the day something gets me, huh?"

Matt looked at Indira almost betrayed as he tried to come up with the words. "You mean you knew? You knew she wasn't making it out and you didn't warn us? You can see that and you knew and you didn't..."

"She can't," Shiraz said from the corner of the room, his fingers still working over the keys. He was embarrassed and uncomfortable admitting it, but he was more worried about what would happen to Indira if she had to deal with them blaming her. "And those three were just the ones that were going to die. I still don't know what the other thing is that I see on the rest of you if you keep this up. That's why she's trying to talk you out of it. Because everything is leading to more people getting killed and taken. And I don't think she can handle much more of that."

Shiraz looked up and met her eyes. She wanted to argue, but ultimately she couldn't. He was right. She really couldn't take much more of it.

CHAPTER 6

DINNER CONVERSATION

THE MEETING PLAYED over and over again in her mind. Damien quietly watching in the background and that betrayal when she admitted Quantum might not be dead. That accusing tone and the implication that she should have done more. Noa looking so defiant when she walked out. Brittany prying for more information that she didn't want to give. Laura getting it out of Matt when she didn't comply. Matt looking like she had personally led Penny and Esther to their deaths. Shiraz of all people speaking up for her. Since the meeting, Shiraz had barely even looked at her.

She needed the night off, but she also needed to figure out a way to calm the hell down so that she could enjoy it.

A glass of water seemed like a good enough way to pass the time before she left. She found her father coming out from the small workroom off the garage, wiping his hands clean of the oil, and she grabbed him a glass before he said anything. He looked calmer and happier than she'd seen him in years. She knew he was. For the first time, he wasn't afraid that he was going to be kidnapped or taken away in the middle of the night. His lab wasn't under threat of being destroyed or broken into. He wasn't going to be unemployed at any moment because of some mess that wasn't his fault and left trying to come up with the funds to pay for the things his family needed. He was happy. Mostly.

"What's wrong with you?" he asked. "You've been walking around like the world is ending the past few days. And for once, we're in a place where that doesn't happen. Are you still sad about your friend that left town to find her mother? Have you heard from her?"

Indira shook her head and drank her water. He had no abilities, but somehow he wasn't as badly affected by whatever made people forget in Whitten as most people, and she was grateful for it. "No, no one's heard from Penny yet," she said. "I don't know if she's going to come back."

"Too bad," her dad said. "I liked her. But if not her, is it your other friend? The one who died? What was her name?"

Indira shook her head and kept her eyes on her water. She couldn't bring herself to say it again. It still stung too much after yesterday, too many people who knew her echoing it back at her with bewilderment like she had just been some random person they passed in the halls. "She's gone," Indira told him. "There's nothing I can do about that, right?"

"You can still be sad about it," he told her. "She was your friend and now she's gone. There's reason to be sad. You don't have to be okay with it right away. So long as it isn't that boyfriend of yours."

Indira snapped up, looking at her father with wide eyes as he grinned back at her. "I don't..."

"Don't think you can keep things from me like that, Indi. I'm your father. I'll always know."

"Mom told you, didn't she?" Indira asked.

"Yeah." He laughed. "But she thinks he is a nice boy and she hasn't seen him do nothing bad yet, so I will trust him for now. But your mother is worried about you. She thinks you're going to not be very happy soon." His brow furrowed as he said it, trying to remember exactly how her mother had phrased it. "So if this boy is giving you any trouble..."

Indira shook her head. "It's okay, he's good," she said. "It's probably just school or something. With the Welcoming Committee, I'm dealing with a lot of stuff. I probably should have taken a spare this year, but I thought I could handle it. I probably just need to take it a little more easy than I have been. I'll be okay, really."

"I know you will. It's your mother. You know how she worries."

She could see that he was worried as well, though his worry was still that this boy she'd found wasn't quite as good as she claimed he was. Truthfully, Indira knew Kyle was probably for the best right now. He was okay with her hanging out with his best friend alone and didn't think she was going to cheat on him. He thought of her like a hero with a secret identity rather than, well, what she was actually doing. "I know, Dad," Indira said.

He gave her a small hug and shook his head at her, a smile still on his face as he did so. "If he gives you any problems, you tell me," he said, nodding to her mother who looked ready for a night out. Her father excused himself and went to clean up as her mother watched him go.

"Your father talked to you?" she asked.

Indira nodded. "I'll be okay," Indira told her. "It's probably just stress or something. You know how I take on too much."

Her mother shook her head. "There is something coming in your future," she said, that glimmer in her silver eyes letting Indira know that she wasn't joking this time. "Your brother and I, I know we are going to have to leave soon. I haven't mentioned it to your father yet. It has to do with your Uncle and they still haven't spoken to each other, but I'm going to be taking Shiraz with me to visit him. And while we're gone—"

"Wait, what do you mean you're going to see Uncle Ness?" Indira asked, keeping her voice low and trying to hide her panic. "Did you actually see yourself going to join him somewhere?"

"Oh no, I'm just messaging your father to tell him that Shiraz and I are going to be visiting him for a while. I hope it's not important, but you never know when I'm bringing your brother. But while we're gone, something is going to happen with you and we won't be able to help you. I need you to be careful, okay? Whatever it is, be careful."

"I'll be careful," Indira said, with none of the other assurances she usually granted a statement like that. "I promise, I'll do my best to be safe. Whatever it is, I'll try."

Her mother seemed to take that. She nodded and straightened back up. "Okay," she said. "Now you go. Have fun with your boyfriend and try to survive dinner. His father will be talking a lot, but try not to be rude and stay on your phone the whole time."

"I won't," Indira said. "You both worry so much." Still, Indira smiled. It was going to be okay, or so she told herself. As much as she was worried about everything happening right now, she was going to be okay and she just needed to get through the evening. She didn't have to figure out every detail of what she had to do. She could wait until at least after seeing Kyle.

KYLE'S MOTHER GREETED her at the door as she made Kyle set the table for dinner in the dining room. She smiled and ushered Indira in, complimenting her and this time allowing her to take her shoes off at the front door. His mother still wore a pair, but she said nothing about them as she followed her in.

"Hey," Kyle said as soon as he saw her. He dropped the utensils on the table, but his mother was quick to wave him back to work, looking sharply to the knives and forks now scattered on the table. Indira covered her smile as Kyle sheepishly went back to work.

"Come on, dear, give me a hand," his mother said, Indira falling in step behind her and going into the kitchen. "Will is going to be a little late tonight, but that's all right. You don't mind waiting just a little until he comes home, do you?"

"That's fine, Mrs. Hollins," Indira said.

"Oh please, call me Kristie," she said. "And since we have a moment, would you like another cup of tea to tide you over?" She smiled conspiratorially, wanting to take it as a chance to better get to know her before her husband took over the conversation again. Indira was more than willing to oblige, even if she could already see the questions forming on her mind as she began.

She passed Indira a cup of tea and took one for herself, leaning over the side of the island to get a better look at her. "You have such striking eyes," she said, her own brown ones looking back at her. "Does that run in your family? They really are beautiful."

Indira knew enough to look a little embarrassed at the statement. "Thanks," she said. "Everyone on my mom's side of the family ended up with grey eyes. My brother got them too. It's recessive, but my grandmother used to say that their genes were much more persistent."

"And a good thing too," Kristie said with a smile. "You don't see eyes like yours much at all." Indira pointedly ignored the lingering part of that sentence that she was carefully leaving out. Not on someone as dark as you. She was grateful that she knew not to say it, at least. "So you said your father was in robotics?"

"Yeah, he works for a company downtown. Mom's a project manager in uptown, though, I think. Some small tech firm. She doesn't really get to talk about work much because it's always these classified projects, you know? So we just never know what it is exactly, but she seems to like it."

"Oh, well that must be exciting!" Kristie said. "How long has your family lived here?"

It wasn't meant to be offensive, Indira knew, though she had to work to keep her smile loose. She knew what Kristie meant. "My family moved here from England just after I was born," Indira said. She neglected to mention her parents were married after that point, or that she was very likely the main reason her mother was summarily disowned from the family. It was not a happy time, though Uncle Ness had taken the opportunity to come with them and established himself as soon as he got here. "What about you?"

"Oh, we've been here forever," Kristie said dismissively. "Didn't move into Whitten until Kyle was in elementary, though. What was it, third grade? Oh, he was so cute."

"Please don't, mom," Kyle said, joining them more as a protective measure for himself, though he intended it as a way to protect Indira from his mother. Now he was worried about pictures from his younger years coming out and it looked like his mom was more than ready to bring out her phone and show them to her. "I'm begging you."

"Aw, no baby pictures?" Indira asked, a playful smile on her lips as she looked back at him.

The front door opened and Kristie got a wicked grin on her face. "I'll send them to you later if you want them," she said with a wink. She straightened up and shooed the two of them out of the kitchen. Indira followed Kyle out, though even he wasn't quite sure what he was supposed to be doing right now either.

Indira caught a glimpse of Chief Will Hollins as he made his way upstairs, his heavy shoes clunking against the carpet as he walked. She couldn't remember what he looked like until this moment, but one look brought it back in stunning clarity. He was a lot more intimidating standing up and without his glasses. She could tell where Kyle got his height from, as well as his broad back. He didn't wear glasses right now, though there was something else very different about him today that hadn't been true before.

She could hear him. The ambient thoughts, the annoyance at the things he had to deal with, the irritation at having to play nice for his wife and talk to his son's girlfriend, it was all there and readily on the surface. She could hear everything he was thinking and there was nothing he was doing to hide it this time.

Indira's mind started spinning with the possibilities. It might be a trap somehow, she knew, but there was a chance here. People were ready to revolt and get themselves killed, but if she could find out something tonight to convince them otherwise, she might be able to stop this. Part of her wondered if she could dig out a way to get Penny free without having to risk anyone. If she was careful about it, if she could find out the right information, then maybe she could find a way to fix all of this. At the very least, she could stop everyone from getting themselves killed.

She finally almost had something. Finally.

"Sit," Kristie told them, ushering Indira to the opposite side of the table from Kyle. Indira sat down and looked at him, not really sure what she was supposed to do. He didn't seem bothered by it, this apparently being normal. She tried to ask with her eyes what she should be doing here, but he waved her off. She was doing fine, apparently.

Kristie brought out plates already filled with food, setting them in front of Indira and Kyle before going back into the kitchen. Indira ignored them as his father came down, dressed much more casually now as he took his seat at the head of the table. He looked back and forth between Kyle and Indira, his eyes eventually settling on Indira.

He didn't know what to say to her and he didn't really want the conversation, Indira could tell. He would rather it was only his own family and he had no intention of getting to know her better, much more interested in something that was happening at work that he wanted to talk about. Indira would be sure to oblige. His work and his plans were of particular interest to her tonight.

"Hello Mr. Hollins," Indira said.

"Indra," he said. "I see he hasn't scared you off yet."

"It's Indira, Dad…"

"Hasn't yet," Indira said brightly.

Kristie gave her husband a light slap on the shoulder as she set his food down on in front of him. "Be nice," she said. "We have company tonight."

Indira looked down at her food and found that she was going to have to take that advice as well. Though she knew to keep her face neutral, she wondered just what Mrs. Hollins had actually done when she was preparing this meal. It looked like she had boiled the chicken breast on the plate until there was no flavour left in it and paired it with potatoes and vegetables that were equally bland. She couldn't even spot any pepper on the plate or the table.

"I came home, didn't I?" he said with a grunt. "I need to head back in later tonight."

"Is there that much to do?" Indira asked. She got the irritated glare from him and continued, shrinking a little as she explained herself and trying to look apologetic for speaking out of turn. "I mean, Whitten seems like a pretty safe place. I didn't think you'd need to be pulling the crazy hours the cops in Vancouver do."

There was a flicker of a smile across his lips as she said it. The annoyance faded into curiosity.

Kyle flickered with irritation. "It's the expansion project, isn't it?" he asked. "They want to bring the program Whitten has to Dagenham."

Indira risked cutting into the chicken. At least it was cooked through, even if it looked incredibly bland. "How do you actually implement a program like that?" Indira asked, brow furrowed as she tried to figure it out. "I know there's already heroes and villains out there. I mean, you pass the law and that might make the heroes stop, but—"

"Don't make me laugh," Will said, talking around the food as he ate. "At least when you're dealing with the types who know they're breaking the law, they know what the score is. Those self-proclaimed heroes were a much bigger problem when the law passed here. Kept insisting that they'd just stick around long enough to put the bad guys away and fade out, like the laws didn't even apply to them. Oh, just trying to help out. Just want to do one more thing. I needed to help this woman cross the street by punching a building over. You must know how it is."

Indira nodded politely as she ate, taking in the mood of the rest of the table. Kyle was unhappily glaring at him between bites, not at all happy to hear heroes slandered like that. Kristie was must more upset that they weren't focusing on Indira and learning more about her, but she knew better than to interrupt her husband when he was ranting.

Mr. Hollins was where most of her attention was — and not only because this was the blandest chicken she had ever eaten. She gave into her temptation just a little and prodded gently at his mind, trying to see if there was any guard up there at all. She could find something there, some lingering thing that kept her from getting too deep into seeing his thoughts without tipping something off that she was there...

Whatever had been keeping his thoughts hidden before was gone now, and Indira was having trouble not giving into the temptation to probe deeper.

"We were lucky that Whitten came with the infrastructure to handle it. We just had to replace a few pieces and make the parts a little more modern, but it turned out to not be as bad as we were expecting. Villains were easy enough to get rid of, but the heroes were trickier. They keep insisting that they are just going to help out and they mean no harm, but if you keep them around, they tend to attract more of the less savoury ones and it just keeps going. But, like I said, Whitten had the infrastructure to handle it."

Indira kept her eyes from glancing around the room to check for blinking red lights embedded in the walls now coming to life. She kept her body relaxed, but her attempts to look into his mind halted at the fear of being watched. She had to remind herself that the eyes actually on her were much more terrifying and could do far worse than those constantly listening specks.

And this terrifying man was confirming things that she already largely suspected, and would confirm more if she could focus. Namely, that by infrastructure, he meant that he was piggy backing on the technology left behind by Dr. Dalus. The towers were spreading the signals and the specks were doing some things as well. He was very proud of those, whatever it was they were doing, and there was something else. Something a little organic and twisted about replacing parts, but she didn't dare press any further to figure out what that meant yet.

"So it's not going to be easy to move it into another city?" Indira said. "It sounds like it took a lot of work to even set up."

"Oh, we can do it," he said. "It's just been a matter of working out the logistics and trying to repeat the system. Once we've got it and the budget worked out, though, we should be able to set it up just about anywhere that wants it. It just means we'd have to retrain the force of wherever we end up to make sure they know how to handle the initial process, but once that's done, it basically runs itself. Then you aren't going to have to worry about any more of this powers testing I know they're trying to put in place."

He was also radiating hatred along with his pride. He was glad that he was getting rid of any opportunities that would come up for heroes to even spring up. He knew precisely how far reaching the system was and he was happy to be rid of anyone with powers in Whitten so that he wouldn't have to deal with them. He saw them as an aberration, people who were too arrogant for their own good and who believed they were better than everyone else. He wanted them gone for good and making them unable to use their powers and live like regular people was just as good as getting rid of them. So long as he never had to see them again and he could make them disappear if they dare tried to act on their abilities, he was happy.

But there was another thing there, darker and hidden below that. The project had been stalled. The budget to repeat the program wasn't the issue. There was something with the current system in Whitten, something about it that needed to be addressed first. She tried to see more, but she could feel something in there, protecting those secrets from anyone who might seek to peer in.

"It's a little limited," Indira agreed, looking back to Kyle. He kept looking at her like she was betraying him, but she offered him a small smile and a shrug. "People slip through the tests. They can't test everyone and people develop differently."

"Oh, don't mind Kyle," Mr. Hollins said, clearly liking Indira a lot more than his own son at the moment. "He just wants to have heroes back around. I tell him he can get them when he moves out. Then he can go anywhere he wants and get his house destroyed as often as he needs to. He's never had to deal with what it's actually like to have them around and messing up everything you've worked for."

Indira smiled politely as Kristie started to speak loudly. "So Indira, how is dinner?" she asked, glaring across the table at her husband. He grunted, but looked satisfied with himself and he was certainly approving of Indira. She was, as far as he was concerned, a good decision and had the chance to set his son straight about this whole mess of ideas he had about superheroes.

"It's great," Indira said, making a show of finishing it off. It was the blandest thing she'd ever eaten, but she did her best to smile through it, letting Mrs. Hollins talk about just how she'd been working on it all day and wasn't sure what Indira would like. Indira did her best to assure her it was fine, though she knew the reason for the chatter was just to ensure her husband didn't have another chance to talk about work again.

Kristie managed to keep her husband silent like this through the rest of dinner. Kyle relaxed across from her as Indira was asked to recount stories about herself and how she was adjusting to Whitten. They barely noticed when Mr. Hollins left, Kristie deep in a story about Kyle when he first moved here trying to make friends with kids in elementary school. With him gone, Indira let herself relax into the easy conversations and enjoy the colour that flushed through Kyle's face through dessert.

"How about you two go for a walk or something?" Kristie suggested gently as Indira picked up her plate at the end of the meal. She took the plate from Indira and continued clearing the table herself. "Take some time to see each other at least a little tonight."

"And here I was hoping for those baby pictures," Indira said, looking playfully at Kyle.

"We'll get out of your way, Mom," Kyle said quickly. He gently ushered Indira closer to the door before his mother could change her mind. Indira laughed, though let him guide her away. She put on her shoes and jacket as he did the same. Hand in hand, they went out into the cool evening, the sun still out as they wandered toward downtown.

CHAPTER 7

THE SPECKLED CITY

KYLE LIVED ONLY a few blocks from Whitten's downtown. The streets got gradually more busy the further they walked, people peppering the streets to celebrate the end of a hard week and to kick off their weekends. It was still early, the sun only starting to set as the spring stretched into summer, and the cool of the night was not so cold as it had been even a week ago. Still, it wasn't so warm that Indira didn't see fit to slide up next to Kyle as they walked.

"Look, I'm really sorry about my dad," he said. "I think something's gone wrong with his little project and he's been obsessed about it."

"It's fine," Indira said. She had an idea of what might have gone wrong, at least, though she was kicking herself for not thinking to try and pry other things out of him. She wanted to know what was in that white room, and if they were keeping these people alive in there. If there really were people in there at all. What was in there and how did it do all of that stuff to her. Who Iris was. "He's not so bad."

"Well, he seemed to like *you*," Kyle said. He didn't realize how bitter he sounded. He wasn't happy about his father's approval of her, that much was clear enough on his face. "He wants to make the whole country like Whitten. It's like his masterpiece. He really thinks he can do it, too. And he's been getting all these offers from places that are trying to become hero-free to match Whitten and everything. At least it's stalled."

"He can't do it everywhere, anyway," she said. "He's not wrong about the heroes, though. They're stubborn. They want to help and feel compelled to keep helping, even if it's illegal to step in. I mean, it's not that they're trying to break the law or anything, but there are a lot of them who like to do things according to the greater good. And a lot of the time it *does* work out, but there's times when it doesn't really pan out the way people thought it would and a lot of people get hurt. But he's not going to be able to get all of them."

Around them, Indira could tell the specks were listening. Red danced out of the corner of her eye, reminding her that they were always there, embedded in every wall and the ground around them. Whitten was always listening, waiting, and Indira needed to remember to watch her words.

"You sound like you think it might still work sometimes," Kyle said.

Indira shrugged. "They'd have to actually get the law passed, too. I know it would never happen in Vancouver. Everyone loves them too much and almost everyone has a story about how they met one for something at some point and it was the best thing ever. The people who aren't for them are kind of outliers. So he'd have to probably go into a place where they're kinda sucking in order to get the law even passed in the first place."

"I don't know what his problem with them is! Mom said it's something to do with what happened to Aunt Tess, but he barely even looks at her when she's over."

"Well, if something's stalled, then he can't do it, right?" Indira squeezed his hand and leaned into him. "The rest of the country will be safe for a little longer."

Kyle didn't say anything, but he started to relax.

"Any idea what's stalling it?" she asked. "Maybe it will get stalled indefinitely."

"I don't know. Something to do with the system needs replacing. He won't talk about it at home, but I heard him yelling something about infrastructure once. I'm pretty sure all they need to do is replace a part and then he can go right back to this expansion."

Indira blinked, a frown tugging at the corner of her lips. "A part?"

"Something to do with how they find out if there's someone doing hero things. He says you can't trust people to report illegal stuff when it comes to heroes, so he found another way to find out if someone's trying to save people."

She thought his father meant legal infrastructure, not something physical. It raised a very different question, one that she hadn't thought to ask before now. After so much focus on trying to keep everyone alive and trying to think of a way to get people back that Whitten had taken, she never thought of how it had happened in the first place. The story was that the laws were passed and then heroism was banned, but she knew that couldn't be all there was to it. As Chief Hollins had pointed out, heroes didn't just leave. And, as she was constantly reminded of with every black speck embedded into the city, there was a way to quickly get rid of them.

"You know, I could do it," Kyle said after a long silence passed between them. Indira could feel his mind shift as something else was starting to barge in. Something familiar. Indira looked around for a sign of Estelle lurking somewhere in the streets, but Kyle kept talking. "I bet if I became a hero, my dad wouldn't be able to stop me from doing it. What's he going to do, arrest his own son?"

"Kyle, what actually happened to the heroes?" Indira asked. It was out before she could think of a different way to phrase it and she could see the specks flash in recognition of the word. "Did they just get locked away somewhere or did they get packed and shipped away? Do you know how your dad actually got rid of them?"

Kyle hesitated, his memory working hard to recall the days between having heroes and not having them. Confusion flickered across his face, settling into anger as he shook his head. "What does it matter? They aren't here anymore and that's all my dad cares about."

Indira opened her mouth to say something, but there was someone nearby thinking very loudly about her, the thoughts tinged with panic and indecision. She let her attention split, half of it staying with Kyle as he fumed and tried to think of ways that he could be a hero just to spite his father. She knew she should put an end to that thinking, but she doubted he would actually build up the nerve to do anything about it soon. Right now, she needed to find out what was going on.

What she found was Noa, knowing full well that Indira was going to get mad at her for what she was doing. She'd come across something and felt sick about continuing to just walk past people in trouble. She didn't know what Indira's problem was, that she could act just this once. So long as she kept quiet and the specks didn't hear any of the words, then it would be fine. They might be listening, but if she was silent and quick, they would do nothing.

You're going to get yourself killed if you do it, Indira said. *Just call the cops. It's not worth it.*

Make me.

Noa kept moving and making it difficult for Indira to see what she was up to. She knew she had that belt out again and was currently phasing through walls, following behind a pair of men that were walking down the street. It would have been hard enough to see her like this under normal circumstances, but she caught a flicker of something familiar.

Noa, did you... It was a stupid question and she knew better than to ask. She'd changed, adopting the alter ego she'd left behind before she entered Whitten. If Indira could get to her before she did anything, she was taking that damn power belt from Noa and locking it up somewhere she couldn't get to it again. *Noa, it's not worth it. Just call the cops. It's not too late to turn back.*

I can't keep hiding anymore, Indira. We don't deserve this. Besides, so long as we're careful, there's no reason we can't do this.

Indira directed Kyle through the streets as he kept talking to her. Indira was physically on autopilot and he didn't notice as she brought them closer to where Noa was. If she could just get there, Noa might turn back. If she could just look at Noa and get close enough, maybe she would give this up. *I'm almost there. Just... Noa, it's not too late to turn back.*

Not a chance, Noa told her, sounding happy about her defiance as she moved through to another area despite the fear that was also coursing through her. *I haven't been able to do this in years. It's about time I got back into it!*

A strangled yell pierced the twilight. Kyle's absence from her side brought her back to herself, knowing Noa was headed right for it as well. They were only steps away from where it was happening. Indira rushed forward to Kyle's side, finding two men in an alley with a man defending himself with a briefcase. They were trying to attack, but it had proved fruitless so far thanks to the briefcase. At least, until they pulled out the switchblades.

Kyle started to move forward when Indira grabbed him and forcefully pulled him back. "What are you doing?" she demanded, quiet enough that they wouldn't be heard. In the alley, she could see flashes of red as the specks listened and watched.

"I can—"

"Go get the cops!" Indira said, shoving him down the street towards a parked police vehicle. "They are *right over there!* You aren't getting stabbed because you've got something to prove, Kyle!"

He stared at her for a moment before he finally left. Indira stayed, watching from around the corner as Noa stepped onto the scene, dressed in uniform. Indira's stomach dropped at the sight of her. She was in a full suit, a skirt over top of it and boots that reached just under her knees, wearing a purple and white combination to match the white and purple belt that carried her power gems. She carried herself like a hero and she looked more comfortable there than Indira had ever seen her before.

She was going to die. It was probably already too late.

There's already specks watching you, Noa. Get out.

"Shut up, I know what I'm doing!" Noa snapped at her, letting her location be known to the men with the knives. The man on the ground clutched his briefcase as she swung her hand wide. Both of the knives flew out of their hands and into hers. She threw the blades to the side. "Wrong town, guys. You have no idea what you're dealing with."

"It's a fucking hero!"

Indira let her shoulders drop as she turned away from the alley. She didn't need to see what happened next, but she still heard everything in stereo as she refused to let her go alone. Even if Noa didn't know it yet, even if she refused to listen to what Indira told her, she wasn't going to be alone at the end.

"Now leave hi—"

Her words were cut off by a scream as the specks unleashed their fury. Lasers came out of them, ripping through her from several angles. Each speck in the area came to life with a precision point directly on her. Noa dropped to the ground, even her scream dying in the air as one went through her throat.

I'm sorry, Noa, Indira said to her quietly as she dropped down to the ground against the wall. The two men ran out past Indira, both yelling incoherently about what happened in there. Indira sat against the wall and tried to stay with Noa in her mind until she faded away completely. She kept her head down, arms wrapped around her knees and sitting on the pavement, ignoring the police officers who came to arrest the two men who ran out, or the businessman who came out afterwards, looking confused and unsure of what had happened to him.

She wasn't sure when Kyle appeared next to her, but he managed to pull her up as the cops come around for questioning. He could see she was shaking, eyes red and trying to hold back the tears. Kyle convinced them to let her go for now. Gingerly, he put his arm around her and walked her back to his house as Indira tried not to pay too much attention to the white van that pulled up to the alley, or the familiar men in hazmat suits who came out of the back. No one around them took notice of it at all.

This wasn't working. Trying to lay low and survive wasn't going to work if they kept going off and getting themselves killed. She was going to have to let them do something. Noa had been there for so long and tonight was the night she decided that enough was enough. And now she was gone.

Indira was so sick of watching people she knew die over and over again. It had to stop. She just needed it to finally stop before everyone else met the same end. She was going to need a plan and help. And if she was going to actually let people help her, she would have to choose her people very carefully.

CHAPTER 8

RALLYING THE TROOPS

"SOMETHING HAPPENED," MATT said as they walked to the Welcoming Committee room. After months, he was finally off the crutch, though he still walked slowly as his legs were getting used to bearing their own weight once more.

"Something's always happening," she said. "You're going to have to be a lot more specific than that."

"You've been off since the weekend," he said. "We lost someone, didn't we?"

"Noa. Grade ten. She'd been here a while, too, but I guess that makes my count four for the semester."

The name sparked something in Matt's memory. There was someone there for him, though she felt like a distant and fading memory. There was also worry for Indira, and the embarrassment at having relied on her to keep Penny from drawing on him so much. It was helping him heal, so Indira didn't mind, though he was starting to think she should stop.

"You're doing too much, Indira," he told her. "You need to take it easy. You're starting to burn out."

"I'll be fine," she said, pushing open the door and letting herself in. "I've just been trying to figure out how to work this out, though. There's a lot more information than I had before, so I just need to figure out what I'm supposed to do with it all."

"Which is why you're calling a meeting," Matt said, dropping his things next to the couch that he'd essentially commandeered since the new year. He really was looking better, though she could still see Penny draining on him now and then. She could also see that Matt was trying to block her influence on his own now.

She dropped into a chair across from him, glancing up to see Shiraz's machine still working. "I found out where the specks came from. I know how they work. I know where they're keeping the people they take, and I know how they're silencing people. I also learned that they are trying to expand this program outside of Whitten. Meaning if it doesn't stop here, it's spreading to the rest of the country where they can. It sounds like we've got some time, but who knows how long. I just... we need to do something. For everyone we've lost already."

More people trickled in, a small section of those who had been there the last time. Indira had chosen them this time, asking Shiraz if any of them were about to die before asking. They heard the conversation and stayed quiet, listening in and watching as they took seats around the room. Indira didn't look, not breaking her conversation with Matt as she turned over what she needed out of them in her head. She didn't know what she wanted out of this beyond a loose idea of feeling like they were doing *something*.

"Do you think we'll be able to get anyone back?" Matt asked, not really hiding the hope and fear of her answer.

Indira shook her head. "I'm not holding out hope. But I think we are going to have to go back in there and find out exactly what's in that room and figure out what to do to take it down. There's something wrong with whatever is keeping Whitten like this, I think. Kyle seems to think it's just a part they need to replace, but I'm betting it has something to do with that white room that we couldn't get close to."

"Could something be wrong with Iris?"

"You are going to have to back right the hell up," Brittany said, leaning in and glancing back at the door. Damien took his cue and locked it before taking his own seat, the room now filled with only those Shiraz had said were not going to die any time soon. Indira hoped that meant telling them this wouldn't change that. "Starting with why the hell you're okay with doing this now when you were so adamant against it before."

"Noa," Indira said. "Grade ten. I kicked her out of the meeting last time along with Scott and Cheryl. She decided she couldn't live in hiding anymore and decided to stop a mugging. And then she lost her life to the damn specks. It doesn't matter how hard we try, people keep doing that. And she's been here a while. She knew and decided she couldn't take it anymore. How much longer before it happens again?"

Her gaze shifted pointedly to Ronnie, who she knew had been thinking of doing the same thing. He avoided her eyes and the room shifted uncomfortably. Damien was already antsy. Though Alan was quiet, Indira knew that he was less than willing to live in hiding like this either. He wanted freedom, as did the rest of them. At the very least, they didn't want to be scared anymore.

"So I've been doing some digging. Sort of. I ended up getting a peek in Chief Hollins' head and I learned that they're planning on expanding the program. I found out a little about how he did it here, which is a bit more of a starting point."

"Don't tell me," Matt said, shaking his head.

"Yep," he said. "Villain technology. Your guess was right on with that one. The specks aren't inert at all. And it's not just that some of them are listening. They can do a few other things too that I've neglected to mention."

"You mean the laser thing?" Ronnie asked. He shrank as the other eyes around the room turned on him. "What? Didn't anyone else mention that part yet? I mean, I didn't know about it until a couple months ago, but I kinda figured everyone knew about it. Shiraz figured it out before I did and it's not like he can really do much, right?"

Something struck Indira from inside her head, like someone was trying to get in touch with her. She looked around the room, noting very sharply that Shiraz was not actually here. She reminded herself that she hadn't asked him to show up today, but something felt wrong.

"What do you mean *lasers?*" Brittany demanded as Ronnie continued to back away. She turned on Indira instead. "*Lasers?*"

She should get out of there and see what that was. Shaking her head, she tried to get up. "I have to—"

"Oh no you don't," Brittany said, pushing her back down. The feeling of someone trying to get her attention was gone, but she was left with a lingering feeling that she should check on that. "What the hell does he mean by lasers? What did your brother find out and just never bother to let the rest of us in on?"

"It's the speck things, right?" Damien asked. Brittany rounded on him next, Laura finally making it to her side and putting a calming hand on her shoulder. "What? I can figure this shit out too. They wait for keywords, then they start listening and turn into cameras, right? And if the cameras see anything, they laser out and kill anything that looks like someone using powers."

Brittany narrowed her eyes on him. "How do you actually know that, though? Her brother's taken those things apart and built shit to block them out, so him I buy, but how do you know that?"

He smiled at her. "Because I'm just that amazing."

"He's a nullifier," Indira said. "But didn't you get locked after the last powers test?"

Damien stared at her with his mouth open, trying to put the words together. "How do you even know that?" he demanded. "*No one* is supposed to know the results of those."

"Apparently Indira cheated the test," Laura offered.

"You can't *cheat* the powers test!"

"We're getting nowhere," Indira said. Still, she felt like she was supposed to see about whoever had been calling to her.

"We're not done," Damien insisted. "How do you know about my powers test?"

"*I read minds, Damien,*" Indira told him. She knew well before that, having been one of two people who had sent Uncle Ness his way. "And I'm seeing that you saw someone die by lasers from the specks."

Damien looked far from done, but the eyes on him made him hesitate. "There was this guy downtown," he told the room. "A contact of mine. We were supposed to be working together to figure out where some people went after they came to Whitten, but he's… not around anymore. I watched the police tape off the area, then the guys in hazmat suits took him away, and then it was like nothing ever happened."

Indira nodded at him. "Welcome to Whitten," she said. "Get used to that. I'm sorry, but you and me and a few other people are the only people who are ever going to remember when something like that happens. I don't quite know how, but they have something set up so that the whole city just never knows or remembers when someone goes missing."

"Or murdered in the middle of the street?"

"Welcome to Whitten," Indira repeated coldly. She was feeling anxious about getting home, but she wasn't going to be able to with this many people watching her. "If you came in with any new information, now's the best time to bring it up."

"You already know I'm looking for Quantum," he said. "*He* was supposed to be checking up on some old friend while he was here."

Matt shot her a look, as did Alan. Alan was the one who spoke. "That name sounds—"

"Yes," Indira told them. "Quantum saved both of you and Penny back on Halloween, but he didn't make it out of there. He might be alive, but I don't know. He's being kept in that place I can't get to, but so are a lot of other people. But I think Penny's in there too and we're pretty sure she's still alive."

"Penny?" Alan asked. He looked sorry for asking as soon as he said it, but he wasn't sure why.

"My sister," Matt told him. "She's still alive. Trust me."

"How can you be sure she's still alive?" Damien asked. "I'm pretty sure my contact is dead, so why would she get to stay alive?"

"Hey Indira?" Ronnie asked, coming to her side now that she had a moment. "What's going on with your brother?"

"What do you mean?"

Ronnie turned his phone around, messages flashing on the screen and vanishing like they were being deleted. Indira took it from him, seeing the messages from Shiraz coming and going, flickering in and out of existence as the connection failed to retain them. Indira gave him his phone back and checked her own, finding there were messages from her mother there as well, flickering in and out of existence for a moment before it stopped completely. Her phone did not alert her to any of them. As they flashed past, she caught one message.

He'll be okay.

Indira got to her feet. "I need to go," she said. Laura held Brittany back and she left, eyes following her as she went. She *knew* there was something wrong before and she had stayed to indulge this for too long. This was a mistake. She should have just gone home instead of filling them in on anything. She didn't even know what she wanted to do with this meeting, and now something had happened. She had to get home.

CHAPTER 9

KEEP CALM

INDIRA MADE IT to the parking lot without anyone stopping her, keys in her hand and determined to get home. The panic was still there, though the reason why was already starting to fade from her. The panic was fading as well, though she clung to it. Something was wrong at home. She had to get home because something was very wrong. Something with... Shiraz? It must be something with Shiraz.

"Indira? Indira, I have to talk to you."

Indira jumped at the voice. She thought she was alone, but she turned, finding Estelle coming for her. "Not now, Estelle," she said, continuing to her car. She had to go while she still remembered what was going on. Why was she forgetting this time when she hadn't any other?

"We need to talk, Indira. Just for a minute, I promise, and then—"

"I said not now," Indira snapped at her, throwing open the door of her car. Her phone vibrated in her pocket and she threw it into her bag, unable to deal with what anyone else wanted of her now. She could feel the worry slipping away from her as Estelle kept talking. She wasn't going to let it happen. She *couldn't* let it happen. She needed to just keep moving and get home before anything else came up and there were more problems. Somehow, she needed to get home.

The reason she was in such a hurry slipped away from her most of the drive home, but once she was there, the panic was back in full. She was kicking herself for not realizing that something was wrong and running to see what it was as soon as Shiraz tried to get in touch with her. He thought he'd be able to see it coming if something were going to happen to him. But he only saw if someone was dying, and only assumed that he would be able to tell if his end was near. There were also a million other things that could happen that were just as bad. Just because he didn't see it coming and mom didn't...

But she did see something coming. She saw that she was leaving town with Shiraz. Indira hoped that it was just that. If something happened to her brother when she wasn't looking — if he'd died from doing something — she didn't know what she'd do. But her mother always knew when someone was going to die in the family, so she would have known about Shiraz, surely, even if he didn't.

She saw a white van driving away from her street as she turned onto it and tried not to worry at what that might mean. It could have been anything at all. It didn't have to be someone there to clean up their mess. There were plenty of other people who drove white vans around the city. Maintenance crews, or anyone who was there for repairs of some sort. And it didn't have to be coming from her house. Indira hoped desperately that they weren't driving away from her house.

The only strange thing she noticed when she came home was that the light over the garage was out. Normally, she rarely noticed that her parents never seemed to turn it off, but now she was looking for things that looked strange. Indira tried to stay calm, but her nerves were starting to get to her as she fumbled for her keys. She stretched her mind inside the house, but she couldn't hear anyone. Her mother's car was gone from the front of the house. She hoped that they were... what? She didn't know what she was hoping for. She just didn't want anyone dead inside.

Indira got in the house and left her shoes at the front door along with her bag and her vibrating phone, going upstairs to find that nothing had been touched. Shiraz wasn't home and his bag wasn't even there, though she'd seen his shoes downstairs. It was odd to see nothing of him left behind, but she tried to calm down. There was nothing here. Nothing unusual except for the fact that there was nothing on in his room at all. She tried the light, but it was already flipped on. The power was out in his room.

Trying to make herself breathe deeper, she forced herself to calm down. She walked through the house to try every light, only to find that they were all not working. In every room, there was no sign that anything was wrong or had been tampered with. Instead, she was left with this lingering doubt, wondering what had happened. She wouldn't accept that both her mother and brother had died, but she couldn't seem to find Shiraz anywhere. She was kicking herself now for not telling her mother what was going on.

She came down to the kitchen and found a note from her mother on the counter. There was nothing hurried or rushed about her neat handwriting, which was a deep comfort, and the page had been neatly torn from the pad before being placed carefully in the center.

Indira,

As soon as I get the call from your uncle, I'll be heading out of town with your brother. Remember to be careful. Your father already knows. I'll call you as soon as we get there.

Love,

Mom

Indira wasn't sure whether or not to be comforted. It didn't explain why the lights weren't working, and her mother still didn't know that Uncle Ness was not going to be in Vancouver. There were people from Vancouver apparently coming here to find him. But at least Indira could believe that they got out of town.

She hated how this was becoming her problem, but there was nothing she could do about it for now. Now that she was feeling calmer, she picked up the phone and found she'd missed even more texts while she was madly searching through the house. Later. She would deal with them later.

She needed to get the power on first, and then she could worry about getting back to the people she'd abandoned less than an hour ago. Indira ignored the messages and called her father. It rang until it went to voicemail and she hung up. She let out a sigh and rested the phone in her hand against the counter, letting her eyes wander around as she waited for him to call her back.

There was something staring back at her. From the corner wall of the living room, she could see a red light coming from behind the paint, the colour so muted that she doubted it would have made anyone think twice about it if the light were on. She couldn't quite shake the feeling that this wasn't the only one that was on right now. With her phone in hand, she started walking through the rest of the house, spotting the odd light coming from the floor or the ceiling or behind the paint. For all her mother tried to get rid of them, they were still there, and it seemed that they were all listening intently.

When her phone rang, she picked up. "Hi Dad," she said, trying not to sound like she was freaking out.

"Indira, your mother left for the city to see her brother," he said. He was at work and sounded like he was in the middle of something. "She took your brother, so you have to find your own dinner tonight."

"The power's out," Indira said, heading upstairs. There were no red lights on in her room or her brother's or the bathroom, but it looked like they were just about everywhere else, spread out and sparse though they were. "Where is the breaker?"

"Same as the old house," her dad said. "Just by the door in the garage. Are you going to be okay?"

"I'm fine," Indira said, almost as an automatic response this time. "Did Mom say when she'd be back?"

"Who knows." She could almost see her dad shaking his head as he was smiling. "She said this morning that she knew she was going to be taking Shiraz with her, so it might be something serious. Otherwise she might have taken you."

"Funny, dad," Indira said. "When are you back tonight?"

"Not tonight," he said. "There's a new contract. We're just getting started. You might not see me for a couple days. For some reason nothing I've been bringing home lately works, so I'm just going to work from here. No boys."

"Did Mom say I was going to bring boys?"

"No," he said. "But don't stay up too late with your friend. You still have school tomorrow."

"I won't," Indira said, frowning as she went to the garage. She had no idea who he meant by that, but that likely only meant that Brittany was going to come by, or Laura would, or maybe both. She would certainly feel better if she wasn't in this house alone for too long without knowing what happened. "Thanks Dad. Good luck with the new contract."

"I'll be home as soon as I can. Bye."

"Bye Dad."

He hung up and Indira went to the garage. The breaker was mercifully easy to find, though it looked like it had been tampered with. The panel was untouched, but there was a hole in the drywall and wires spilling out of it. As she flipped the switches on the breaker, she could hear the house come back to life. There was something comforting about that, but she was worried over the mess of wires. Something was removed from their house and Indira had no idea what it was. She worried that it was the real reason that Shiraz and her mother had skipped town. Particularly since Uncle Ness was definitely still missing and her mother was about to find out just how long he'd been gone.

As she walked back into the house, she couldn't see the specks watching her anymore. She wasn't sure if that was because the lights were hiding them, or if they had gotten bored of watching her. She tried not to think about it, though her eyes kept trailing to every corner and she paid much more attention to the paint.

She went back to Shiraz's room and started scrolling through her phone, trying to decide which text to actually answer. Brittany was trying to be concerned. Laura was actually concerned. Kyle wanted to know if she was free this evening. She texted to tell him that she was going to bed early for now. In the meantime, she found Matt's text asking if she was okay and decided to call him.

"Indira?" he asked as soon as he picked up. "What happened?"

"I think it's okay," Indira said as she went through her brother's room. Nothing was wrong in the house, but Indira knew *something* must have happened. She wasn't even sure if she was supposed to be as worried as she was right now, which was frustrating. It looked off in here, like everything had been carefully reset, the mess intentional rather than Shiraz's carelessness, though she wasn't sure why. It felt like there was someone else was in here. She couldn't quite place what was wrong, but there was something off. Maybe it was the game controllers placed too neatly back in place? "Apparently mom just took Shiraz out of town."

"Why?" he asked.

"To visit my uncle?" Indira asked. She ran her hand over Shiraz's desk, looking around for any sign of the red specks and finding nothing. Now, she just needed to remember how to open the latch for it. "It was pretty quick. I don't really know what's going on."

"Is your dad there at least?" he sounded worried. Indira's hand started to itch, but she ignored it.

"He's working," she said. "And he said no boys, so you're not invited either," she added, forcing a laugh. She needed to keep her spirits up, even if she had to fake it. Even if Matt knew that she was faking it. He was good about making a disappointed sound on his end, but leaving her to continue talking as she finally found the latch. She opened up the secret compartment in Shiraz's desk so she could take a look at his real work. "But apparently someone's coming over tonight to keep me company, so don't worry too much."

"You're making it really hard not to worry about you, Indira," he said.

She struggled to get the compartment open, but it finally started moving. "You're just upset you don't have your own sister to worry about anymore," she said, not intending to be cruel with her words, though it slipped out. It was tough to restrain herself when she saw what was under the desk and she let out a strangled gasp at the sight of it, though she quickly silenced herself.

There was blood under here. Too much of it and it was fresh, spilled across loose circuits and tools. The soldering iron hadn't cooled down completely yet, making the inside warm and the smell of the blood more pungent as soon as it hit her. Her stomach turned. How had she not smelled it before? Whatever had happened, it happened recently.

"What? What happened?"

"It's nothing." She dropped the desk back into place with a bang and locked it.

"I heard that. That wasn't nothing. What's going on?"

"I'll talk to you tomorrow."

"Ind—"

Indira disconnected and put her phone on vibrate for the night. Her hand itched, but she couldn't take any more calls. She had to try and find him, to see for herself that he was actually going to be okay. It might be early still, but she was going to her room for the night and getting some answers.

CHAPTER 10

DEAD ENDS AND LIFE LINES

ON THE BRIGHT side, her hair was going to be fantastic in the morning. With her brush in hand, already working through her long locks to give her a place to come back to, Indira let her mind go wandering. She immediately dove into the few sleeping minds around her, looking for Shiraz and hoping he wasn't too far out of reach yet. She could still feel him there, though he was getting further and further away as the moments passed. As she thought from the amount of blood she'd found in his desk, he was likely unconscious and hopefully stable after whatever had happened.

When she found him, she did not waste time with the polite request to make sure she was allowed in and burst into his dreaming mind. She found him huddled in a ball in the middle of nothing and not moving, images flashing around him dimly as he clutched his shoulder tight.

"Raz!" Indira snapped at him, worried and terrified of what was going on. She was at his side in an instant and grabbed his other shoulder, spinning him around to look at her. "What happened? Where are you?"

"Indi?" he asked. Shiraz looked around, surprised that there was someone else there. He winced as he straightened up. His hands were bloody where he nursed his shoulder, pain flickering across his face, even in this dream. "What's going on? You shouldn't be here." He let out a groan, but there was confusion there as well. Around them, the nothingness lit up to reveal his room. He was sitting at his desk while she stood at the door. "You're staying late, aren't you? And I'm ..."

"You're dreaming, Raz," Indira told him. He was lost in his head and Indira took a deep breath to steady herself. He was hurt from something to do with this damn town and she was going to burn it down as soon as she could figure out how. "Something happened to you, Raz," she said, forcing herself calmer. Right now, she had to find out what happened, which meant Shiraz needed to understand what was going on. "Mom's got you and she's taking you somewhere, but I don't know what happened."

"Right," he said. There were two of him now, one still sitting slumped at the desk in pain, and another more bewildered one looking between him and Indira. His attention settled on the other version of himself, who straightened up and opened the desk to reveal the hidden work station. Shiraz hovered over his memory, watching as he worked and replayed the events over. "I unset the thing on the house that blocks the specks. I wanted to test something, but the power went out. So I tested it anyway. No power means it doesn't work anyway. And then…"

Indira couldn't make out the words Shiraz said, the dream leaving them too muddled, but the specks in front of him flashed red. He stayed quiet and kept working, waiting for them to turn off. Once they did, he tried another string of phrases, texting someone between each experiment.

Their mother appeared in the door as something crashed into his back, slamming him into the chair before he bounced back into the desk. Shiraz didn't see what it was at the time so Indira saw nothing, but she knew it was the specks.

Wasting no time, their mother dove for the desk, pulling Shiraz away from it and grabbing a sheet of metal he'd been working with to cover his back. There was a loud noise of something hitting the metal. The desk slammed shut and their mother dragged him out of the room, Shiraz feebly trying to do something with his phone.

"I think I told her we needed to leave town. I'm not really sure what happened after that. I don't really know why that didn't work though."

Indira didn't stop him as he walked back around the desk and opened it again. There was only one of him now, though Indira worried she wouldn't be able to talk to him for much longer. He was already so far away and getting farther. Indira had to get answers quickly, but he was still too distracted.

Shiraz peered at the device on his desk. There were holes in his back, going through his shoulder and down his spine. Someone had wanted to silence him or get him out of the way, that much was certain, though she wasn't sure why. He hadn't shown off powers or done much other than spout phrases. He wasn't setting off anything other than the listening functions on the specks, was he?

"It wasn't on," Shiraz said, going closer to get a better look at the device on the table. The blood was gone again and he laughed at himself. "I just didn't set this all the way. I closed my desk, right? The specks can't listen when my desk is closed."

"I think Mom's trying to get you out of town," Indira told him. "It's getting really hard to stay here. Tell me you're going to be okay."

"I didn't get any hint of a death mark," he said. "And if Mom didn't catch it, I think I'll survive this. I just don't really know what happened or how bad it is. Dad is going to be pissed when he has to clean up though, isn't he? I know he hated it when Uncle Ness bled on the carpet. I'm pretty sure I was bleeding."

"They came and cleaned it up," Indira told him. She tried to move, just so she could touch him and let herself know he was still there, even if it was only a dream, but she was having trouble staying there at all. "Raz, if she asks, just tell mom everything. And tell her that you can't come back. Don't let her come back and don't you come back either."

"I don't even know where we're going."

"You're going to Uncle Ness' place, I think," she said. "Mom left a note saying you were going there. She should know Uncle Ness is gone before she gets there. If you wake up, just tell her everything. And that I'm sorry I didn't tell her about any of this before."

"I think she's going to be more mad that you didn't try to get us out of here sooner once you found out. Or that I didn't. There's a lot for her to be mad about here. And you're leaving me to deal with it on my own."

"Hey, you're dying. She'll go easy on you."

"Or she'll finish the job." He laughed, light and carefree and comforting. He was getting too far away to hold onto this much longer. He didn't seem to notice it, but he was drifting away, leaving her behind. "You need to get out of there, Indi. It's not safe."

Indira watched as he faded away, glad he couldn't see the expression on her face. Of course it wasn't safe. It hadn't been safe since the day they set foot in this place, but it made their parents happy. And after everything, making them happy seemed like a fine sacrifice. It was fine until they realized that they were going to be stuck there forever and risk dying if they made too many mistakes. Indira had used her powers less when she was under constant threat of kidnapping and getting crushed under falling debris than in the damn Speckled City where they outlawed the causes of most of that.

And she was stuck in it for a little while longer. For all her thinking, she had yet to come up with any solid plans for how she was going to do anything besides warn people to lay low when they came through the halls of Larkdale Secondary. She couldn't come up with a way to get Penny or Uncle Ness out, or how to take down anything that was causing all these problems in the first place. She needed a plan, and she knew where she had to start.

Indira touched back with her body first, noting where she was still brushing her hair and letting herself become just a little more present. Her phone was vibrating on the table next to her, but she continued to ignore it. She just wanted to remind herself where she was and give her one last chance to back out. Knowing her brother's blood was still likely wet in the next room kept her going.

She'd been avoiding that empty lot and the white room under it since the last disaster here, but it was time for her to go back. She didn't need the physical location, only the memory of tragedy to draw her back to the place. If she concentrated, she could still feel the hum of power coming from that room. But she didn't need to try to and see what was in there. Not yet.

The underground facility was different than before. It felt like she was alone now, that Iris was no longer around to keep an eye on her. She was certainly not trying to call her back to the room this time, but that wasn't where it stopped. Though she could still only see the one hallway without Matt's magic illuminating the rest of it for her, she was now aware of the rest of the paths and could push past the illusion hiding them from her. Nothing tried to push them back in place for her, and Indira was free to wander around to her heart's content without a chaperone.

Now that she knew where the halls were, she walked through them, finding that there were people wandering these more frequently. The men in the hazmat suits were still here, but in fewer numbers now, and there were more men without helmets that bore police uniforms or badges clipped to their belts instead. Their eyes were glazed over, their movements just as stiff as those who wore the suits.

Indira ended up in the corner where everything had finally gone wrong. Matt had been shot here. Penny too. And she'd seen Esther get shot and die here, filled with holes. It was her fault for not having looked far enough ahead. It was a reminder that she was going to have to be more diligent this time. And that she might have to do this on her own to keep everyone else alive.

There was a familiar man walking through the hall. She had seen Officer Jericho Nava once before, at Esther's small funeral. He didn't look happy burying his daughter, but she got the feeling he wasn't a man who smiled much under normal circumstances. He was dressed fully in his uniform, but it was striking how he didn't look quite as out of it as everyone else who wandered through the halls. His brown eyes were alert, looking sharply to the men in hazmat suits walking down the hall. With a sharp gesture, they changed their route, going into one of the side rooms.

She knew the man was a cop, but it was still startling to see him down here. He must have known that Esther hadn't been killed in a hit and run like the stories had said. She had died where he now stood, trying in vain to save her friends from Indira's mistakes.

He must know that this — something to do with all of this down here — was the real reason she had died. Surely, he couldn't just be going along with it.

If he even remembered he had a daughter.

As the realization struck her, he walked past the corner, following the hazmat suits away. As he did, that life in his eyes faded away and he became like the rest, his movements stiff and automatic once more. From everything Indira had learned about this place, she always forgot that those who were lost to Whitten, however their ends came, ended up forgotten.

She followed them into one of the side rooms and didn't know what to make of what she saw there. It was a long, narrow space, filled with metal pods lining the walls. The men in the hazmat suits went into the back of the room to remove the suits and Officer Nava opened the door to two other pods, handing the people coming out a pair of suits.

Indira watched, not sure what to make of what she was seeing. She had thought the people in them were dangerous and strangely absent of thought, but there was something else off about them now that she saw them outside of the suits. One that crawled back into one of the pods was covered in marks like he had been shot and it had been healing very slowly. Inside the pods, she saw the faces of people who looked like they were being preserved until they could be put to use once more. Now that she was paying attention, she noted that none of them had any sign of brain activity despite their movements, making Indira wonder just what was making them do anything. It wasn't like their minds were being blocked. They simply did not think. Their brains had gone into a vegetative state as their bodies seemed to be healing from grievous wounds.

And in the pod next to him was Chris. Shiraz wondered what happened to him, had said that he might be that thing other than dead. Indira never quite knew what that meant. He looked like he might be alive still, but his mind was wrong. She tried to reach into it to see if there was anything of him left in there, but there was nothing. As far as his mind was concerned, he was dead, even if his body hadn't caught up yet.

Indira jerked away from the room and got as far away from it as she could. She didn't understand what she was looking at, why it was happening. Part of her could see the sense in it. If there was someone who they needed a little extra muscle to take care of, they had a whole super powered army at their disposal, and whatever spell they had over the town kept people from re-membering the faces they might see inside the suits. But with the specks, was it really necessary to resurrect the dead to keep the order?

Indira didn't stop until she felt something sticking. She jumped as she realized how close she had gotten to the white room and tried to back away from it. She threw herself into her escape and found herself flying away. It wasn't nearly as powerful or insistent as it had been last time. It was like Iris really wasn't there at all, only a memory of her, leaving the area no stickier than a movie theatre floor. She could actually get close now without worrying about getting trapped.

She could take a look inside.

The room was no less powerful than before, though it didn't call to her in the same way. There were voices as she got close to it, the mental screams of people wanting desperately to escape, but she couldn't actually pick out Uncle Ness calling to her. She didn't hear Penny amidst the cacophony of them and, if she didn't pay attention to it all, the voices together became nothing more than noise.

Just one look. She only needed one look. That was what they wanted the first time they came and now she could actually see what was in there. She knew it had driven Matt and Penny mad, but without Iris there, maybe it would be all right. She just needed to see what was in there, just enough to tell if her suspicion was right. If Uncle Ness and Penny really were in there.

Despite the power radiating from the room and the psychic interference making it hard to look at, it was really just an ordinary door. Experimentally, she pulled herself back, finding that she could still get away if she wanted to. It would be fine. She just wanted one look at what was in there.

Indira got close enough to the door and pressed herself through. Immediately, the noise of wailing got louder, latching onto her and pulling at her. They knew she was there, knew she was free, and latched onto her. Some wanted so desperately for her to stay and save them, to get them out of there so they could see their families and the sky again after so long. Others pushed her away, trying to tug her out of their grasp and send her out of there and back to safety. She was pulled in every direction, surrounded by the needs of them all fighting against each other and all of it tearing her apart.

Only one thing kept her from shattering. The sticky white presence of Iris, much more subdued than it had been before, wrapped tightly around her. Where Indira had been trying to be as much of a detached, non-presence there as she could, Iris pulled her completely into the room and held her there in one piece while every other voice around her tried to pull her apart.

She thought she would be trapped there forever, drowning in the voices that tried to break her apart, when she was yanked away. All of her was pulled away, though she felt stretched and disconnected as the voices, pleading and screaming and yelling, all finally fell to silence. The quiet rang in her ears as she tried to pull herself together. Everything about her was shaking, but slowly she made herself whole again.

She wasn't alone. Estelle stood there in this plane, arms crossed and frowning down at her. "What the hell are you doing?" she demanded. "I've got this! You keep doing that and you're going to end up getting stuck in the blob with everyone else!"

"I'm going to see what we're up against," Indira told her. She felt breathless still, even without the ability to breathe when she was like this. Already, questions circled through her mind. "Look, thanks for the rescue, but what the hell are *you* even doing out here? And how did you get me out of there?"

"Because I know how to get people out of my own stuff!" she snapped at her. "You need to stop coming. I've got this."

"What do you mean *your* stuff?" Indira asked, looking her carefully over.

Estelle let out a deep sigh, running her hand over her hair and letting it trail down her braid. "Look, Indira, I need you to back off. You don't even know half of what's going on right now and I'm not always going to be around to pull you out of my head. Or whatever my head has spilled out into. Look, you just really need to stop doing all of this and just let me take care of it, okay? I've got this."

"I have no idea what you're talking about," she said. "Can you back the hell up and tell me just what the hell is going on here? How are you the thing down there and the person up here and, presumably, the person at school as well? Because I think I'm going to need the cliff notes version of whatever is happening." Indira knew plenty about mentally being in several places at once, but this felt like a whole different matter. When Estelle hesitated, looking between angry and desperate, Indira suggested, "The beginning would be good."

"Fine," Estelle said, sitting down on nothing and playing absently with the braid between her fingers. "That white stuff you keep getting stuck in when you're trying to get closer to the core, that's me. Or a part of my mind. It used to be all of me, but then you came along. I never thought of doing that with my powers before, but I managed to fracture a part of myself out of there."

Indira held back her disbelief. That Estelle having been whatever it was in the white room was strange enough to process. That she hadn't known about projection as an option until she'd seen Indira do it was another, far less important matter, even if that was the thing Indira's mind insisted on latching onto.

"I don't even know how long I've been trapped in there," Estelle continued. She was more bitter than depressed about this fact. "This is the first time I've gotten out ever. And I am going to get the rest of me free as soon as I figure out how, but you are not making that easy."

"So you're the one I kept feeling watching me every time I went in there?" Indira asked. "You're Iris?"

Estelle shrugged. "I was going to be. I needed a costume to be a hero, but my brother kept stopping me."

"What are you doing to all those people in there?"

"I'm not doing it on purpose," Estelle insisted. "I don't want to do this to people! I just— One day I'm saving people from a falling building and I broke my lock. Do they still have locks? They're these things they put on people who are too powerful—"

"You *broke* it?"

"People were going to die! I knew I could kinda move stuff, so I tried to save them and I kinda overloaded it and I got stuck in my head for a long time. I could never really get out again. But my brother, he kept talking to me and told me how I could help him. I thought it was for something good. He found something and—"

"Aunt Tess?" Indira asked, looking at her again, though feeling like it was for the first time. She did look a bit like her now that Indira was paying attention. Her hair was much fuller, but she had Kyle's eyes. "But you were at Kyle's house that night."

"Only Will ever called me Tess," Estelle told her. "And, like, I don't think I've left that room in I don't even know how long. I know for a while they were trying to split me or something so they had a second of me? Maybe that's what you saw? I mean, that didn't go well and I don't know how long ago that was—"

"No, it was your body, I think," Indira said. "You *are* Aunt Tess, right?"

Estelle shrugged, confusion crossing her face. "I guess? I must be. Kyle is Will's kid, and Will's my brother, so yeah? I guess I never really thought about it. How long have I been out for? Kyle's older than me."

"Kyle said you were young when it happened," Indira said. She was feeling better with each passing moment and growing more aware that they were getting off topic. And the more Estelle talked, the more Indira realized Estelle knew, even if she was not an active player in any of this. "Do you know why they were trying to split you?"

"Will said he was going to save the world. He still tells me that we're doing good, like I can't hear everyone he hooks into whatever that thing is. They needed another one of me for something, but you can't just duplicate someone, you know? I think. I don't think they ever managed to do it. Which is good, because even if they did, I don't know how they're convincing all these people to hook themselves up into this."

Indira stared at her. "Estelle. No one is going in there willingly."

"I know." Estelle tugged on her braid, shrinking away from Indira. "Will used to tell me he managed to convince them it was to help make it safe. Magic and psychic energy working together to keep the town free of any big supervillains. No heroes, no villains, no people getting crushed by buildings. All I had to do was keep everyone hooked up together and channelling their energies to making it happen, no matter what it took. He has something that makes you believe him. It takes a really long time to see that it's not right. And when you do, you can't stop, no matter how hard you try."

Her knees had come up to her chest as she talked and she looked so small. She stayed silent for a long moment, staring at nothing, but Indira could see her mind working.

"I know he wants to do it again somewhere else," she said at last. "I'm what they need to keep all the psychics and magic people working together. I make everyone not notice when something strange is going on. When they're murdering people in the middle of the day. And then I bring back those that are almost dead, those heroes and villains they try to take down, and I keep them just alive enough so that they can go pick up the corpses and defend the towers. I don't know what the towers do, but they're important."

Estelle let out a breath, her knees dropping in front of her and her eyes falling on Indira. "You have to let me convince Kyle, Indira. It's the only way."

"How the hell is Kyle going to stop any of this?" she demanded. "As much as he wants to be, he's not some hero. What's he going to do, murder you and hope the whole thing falls apart?"

"He's *family*," Estelle insisted. "Will can't go after his son. Kyle's the only one who might be able to go up against him and win. If Kyle starts being a hero, maybe Will can finally figure out that heroes and powers aren't this awful thing he needs to get rid of. Maybe he'll finally let me go. Kyle would do it for me, but you need to let him do that."

"No way," Indira told her. "You think his father is going to stop just for that? Look at what he's done to you! And he tried to figure out a way to cut you in half on top of that! What makes you think he's going to show Kyle any mercy just because he's family? He hasn't given a shit about family so far. Not to mention, Kyle's not going to get this far. How many other people have even gotten close enough to you to talk to you so far, Estelle?"

"He can do it!" Estelle insisted. "He's our only hope! With him, we might even be able to bring back all the people we've lost. Those people that are in the hazmat suits? They're still alive. Barely, sure, but they're technically still alive. We can still bring them back. We just need someone to convince Will to stop what he's doing and who better to do that than his own son? You know I'm right about this, Indira. You have to let him do it."

"Those people are *dead*, Estelle," she said. She was blunt about it and put force behind her words. Indira wasn't powerless here, and she wasn't about to let Estelle push her around. "There's nothing left in their heads. Their bodies might still be moving, but they aren't in there anymore. I don't even know if the people you have in that white room are actually still there or if they're just screaming because that's all they know how to do now. And Kyle's not going to be able to save anyone from that."

"But he's the only chance we have," she insisted. "It's a good plan. All he has to do is show his father what a good thing he's doing and he can convince Will that heroes aren't evil. And once Will knows that, then he can stop. He'll actually listen to his son. He wouldn't listen to me, but people always listen to their kids…"

Indira shook her head. "You're as idealistic as he is," she said. "How old were you the last time you were actually alive? Did you actually know anyone who was a hero? Because it doesn't ever work out like that. Maybe on television, but not normally."

"What are you saying?" Estelle asked. "I'm older than you! I've seen more than you ever will! You think I'm being delusional? This is going to work. It will work because it has to! We don't have any other options!"

"In real life, sometimes you do everything the bad guy tells you and he still kills your parents because there's no reason for him not to anymore. People have to choose between killing the hostages or stopping the bomb from blowing up the city. They let girlfriends die in the flames so that they can protect the city, and they still lose the battle. And I've met Chief Will Hollins. He is not going to back off from taking down and suppressing every hero he can within the confines of the law just because his son is breaking a few of them."

"He will," Estelle insisted. "He will because he has to. *That is his son!* And Kyle will do it. If I ask— If he knew what was going on, he'd do it. It wouldn't even take that much to push him over the edge to make him go up against his father. One little tragedy and he'll put on those tights you hate so much and immediately do everything I ask him to."

Indira caught the look in her eye and the way she was looking at her. Indira backed away, but there was nowhere she could run here "It's not going to work," she told Estelle. "Kyle's going to die if he does it and well before he ever manages to confront his father. There's eyes all over the city and they attack before anyone ever sees a police officer."

"He won't die," she said. "He won't because he can't. But he's going to need something to tip him over the edge and make him do something drastic. And I'm sorry Indira, but you're going to have to be his tragic backstory."

"What, you're going to kill me?" Indira asked, preparing herself. She knew how to defend herself in places like this. She just needed to keep her off balance and hope Estelle didn't realize just how powerful she really was. She just needed to keep her talking and wait for an opening.

"No," Estelle said. The space around them started crumbling away and Estelle faded from view. "I'm just going to leave you here. Because if I remember right, if you wander too far from your body, you have trouble getting back. And you're very far away from your body now, aren't you?"

Indira tried to take a swipe at her, but she was gone, the small contained white room falling away to various thoughts and ideas of the people somewhere around her. She was somewhere in what she liked to think of as the collective subconscious, this part sparsely populated and unfamiliar. She didn't even know how deep in it she was.

Worse, she didn't know where her body was. That familiar motion of brushing her hair was nowhere, Indira left with no anchor back to herself. She didn't even know which direction to go to get back to some physical location she could use as a reference point, much less how to get back home.

After everything, she was so tired. So many things had gone wrong and she wanted nothing more than to curl up and stop forever. No one would even know. Her father said he wasn't going to be home for a while. Even if he did stop in one night, he left early in the mornings. He might not even notice that Indira wasn't getting up and going to school for a few days. Her mother would get the call, but with Shiraz, she might not be able to come back and see what was going on at all. Her friends at school might notice, but they probably wouldn't do anything about it.

But Indira was also needlessly stubborn. Estelle could not go through with her plan. People were going to die, and this time it was going to be someone who didn't even have to be involved. And it would be because Indira didn't get a chance to stop him. She needed to stop Estelle from making Kyle go out and put on some ridiculous tights in order to fulfill a dream he didn't even have.

She had to survive, if only for a little longer. This was why she never wanted to be a hero. Because this responsibility to others was the worst. Now she felt responsible for everyone. Shiraz was hurt and they needed to pay. She needed to get her uncle back. She needed to get Penny back. She needed to avenge Esther.

And so she started walking. She would be able to find her body and she was going to stop Estelle. And she would find some way to stop everything else. She just needed to get back to her body, one step at a time. She would do it because, in the end, she had to.

In the distance, she thought she heard a voice in her ears. She didn't know how long she wandered, but she followed that voice and hoped that it was leading her the right way. As she got closer, she could make out the words that kept calling her so desperately.

"Indira! Come on, I didn't come back for this shit. You are not allowed to do this to me. Indira!"

CHAPTER II

RESURRECTION

EVEN WITH A voice calling her back from wherever she was, Indira was having trouble picking her way through all these thoughts to find the city. There were no physical locations here, only noise and idle thoughts and daydreams of far too many people. She never left Whitten, but beyond that she had no idea where she was.

At least that one voice talking to her body made it through, though it was so distant that it was hard to tell where exactly they were coming from. Worse, whoever it was kept going silent. She had no idea how she was supposed to find her way back with just that. She wished Shiraz or literally anyone from her family was there. They all knew that they weren't supposed to shut up until she got back. At the very least, give her some music to walk toward in all this silence.

But slowly, she got closer until finally she could feel herself again. It was muddy and slow, falling back into her own body, and the trek left her so tired. She wanted to just fall asleep, but whoever it was standing over her wouldn't let her. She was currently shaking Indira by the shoulders and yelling in her face.

"Come on, you aren't allowed to do this to me right now, Indira. I did not do all of this so that you could go and die on me before I even got here. Indira, I swear to god, if you don't wake the hell up soon, I'm going to start cutting off that hair of yours."

Indira knew that voice. Blearily, she opened her eyes, though she couldn't make out the dark mass in front of her at first. Her body was heavy and she wasn't able to quite put together what she was saying. She felt like she had to be imagining it, but as the hands finally stopped shaking her and their eyes met properly, Indira knew that she was actually there.

Esther. Back from the dead.

"Oh thank god," Esther said, her hair falling in Indira's face. There was relief coming off of her, but Indira was still trying to figure out if what she was seeing was real. After the last little while, the stress and the surprises and the turns were getting overwhelming and she didn't know what to make of anything anymore.

Timidly, Indira reached up and found her hands were numb. She hadn't moved in such a long time, it seemed, that everything about her was feeling a little fuzzy. She didn't let that stop her as she touched Esther's face. Esther looked back at her and Indira cupped her cheek, turning her face down so that she could see her better. She wanted to make sure she wasn't imagining this or that this wasn't still somewhere out in the void, where Estelle had tried to come up with something to keep her there longer. Indira would have done it, but Estelle didn't have the skill at it that she did. Esther was warm under her fingers. She was real and she was here.

Her stomach rumbled at her awakening and Indira took her hand back, clamping it over her mouth, eyes wide and alarmed. She turned and scrambled to the door, her limbs weak and moving on desperation to get to the toilet before it was too late. Esther was behind her, muttering calm words in an alarmed tone as she helped get Indira to her feet and half carried her to the washroom.

Indira narrowly made it to the bowl before her stomach emptied. Her hair was pulled back and held behind her, a gentle hand on her back coaxing her through it. She felt nauseous, her head spinning and wondering idly why she would ever want to return to her body again if this was the sort of greeting it was going to give her. She let her cheek rest on the seat as she tried to catch her breath, waiting for the world to quit moving and for her mouth to stop tasting of bile.

"Are you okay?"

Right. Returning to her body had given her something else this time, something that she couldn't have expected. She turned her head to look up at Esther, taking her in as she did something with the sink. It looked like Esther, and the buzzing thoughts around her sounded like she used to. But she was dead. Indira had been there to bury her. "How are you here?"

"It doesn't matter right now," Esther told her. She handed her a cup of water and knelt at her side. "Here."

Indira's hand was shaking when she took it. She took a drink and swirled the water through her mouth, spitting it out along with the lingering taste. "Thanks," she said before drinking the rest.

"Can you get up?"

Indira pushed herself back from the toilet, the dizziness dipping her back toward the ground. Esther caught her and helped her to her feet, draping Indira's arm over her shoulders as she brought her back to her room. She nearly collapsed back onto her bed, curling up on the blankets and trying to make the world stop moving. She let out a low groan, closing her eyes and trying to force everything to stop moving with her mind, though nothing listened.

"I don't know what you were doing, but I hope it was worth it," Esther muttered. She was trying to keep her thoughts quiet, but they pounded loud in Indira's head. And hers weren't the only one.

"Hide," she said.

There was no noise, though she knew Esther had moved. A moment later, there was a knock at her door, her father letting himself in. He turned the light on and Indira cracked an eye open to glare at him from her spot on the blankets. "Dad?" she asked. "Why are you back?"

"Just getting a few things and then heading back," he said. "You look like crap."

"Migraine," she said, offering a weak smile. "It's getting better."

"Maybe stay home tomorrow. Will you be okay? It looks like I'm going to be working on this project for a few days and I don't think I'll be home. And I don't know when your mother and brother are going to be back."

Indira nodded. "I'll be fine. Just need to sleep it off."

"Sleep," he agreed. "Call me if you need anything." He turned the light off and closed the door. Indira didn't move, waiting until she heard the front door close and the car out front start before she tried to push herself back up. The world heaved, but Indira managed to stay upright. She needed an aspirin.

"Can I borrow some clothes?" Esther asked, crawling out from under the bed. "When I went back to my place, Dad packed up all my stuff. Which... I shouldn't be surprised about, really, but it was still weird."

"If it fits," Indira said. She hadn't thought about what Esther was wearing, too distracted by the fact that she was alive now, but it did look very conspicuous. She dressed in black, the colour in her hair gone now and the wild mess pulled back into a slick, low bun. There were patches of skin showing through in spots, though Indira knew that was less for the aesthetic and more so that she had easier access to the flashes of metal hidden just out of sight.

She watched as Esther went ahead and rummaged through her drawers for a change of clothes and frowning at what she was finding. After a few unsuccessful pulls from them, she managed to put together something loose enough that it would fit. Indira paid careful attention to Esther's bare skin as she changed, noting that there was no sign of any mark on her. She also noted that she had quite a few small knives on her that she managed to cover in her new outfit just as easily as her old one.

"You died," Indira finally. Her eyes flickered around her room, finding nothing was triggering at the words yet. "How are you not dead anymore?"

Esther gave her a look before looking around for the lights herself. "You've gotten really careless without me around, haven't you?" she scolded her. "I just got back and you're trying to make me go away again?"

Indira laughed a little and shook her head. "You've missed a bit. Raz managed to make this thing that disrupts the signal so they can't function. We're safe in here."

"Seriously?" she asked, straightening up. She furrowed her brow as she considered it and dismissed it in the end. "That would explain why they're watching your house, I guess. It's the whole house?"

"They're watching the house?"

"I figured it was just because you were still going out with Kyle. You guys are still together, right?"

Indira put her hands up to stop her. Another wave of nausea washed over her, but she pushed it away. "Stop," she said. "You're back from the dead. How are you not dead? You have a grave."

Esther let out a groan. "God, I know," she said. "It took me three goddamn lives to get out of that thing. What, you didn't think I was just hanging out with you guys and helping you along for shits and giggles, did you? I actually *do* have a stake in this. Unfortunately,

Dad looks like he's too far down shit creek now and I don't think I'm going to be able to go home this time around."

"Your dad is working for Chief Hollins, you know," Indira told her. "Not just as an officer. He's working down in that thing with the hazmat guys and the weird room too."

Esther shook her head. "I'm not surprised. He hasn't been in his head since he started working here." She shook her head and sat down. She crossed her legs on the computer chair and spun around to look at Indira. "So backstory time. When Dad started here, it's because he was scouted. Hollins thought he'd be a good fit for the higher up positions because he's always been really tough on heroes who break the law, but I don't think he realized dad's also really light on henchmen types. He used to be one; that's how he met mom. So once he gets the job here, he's happy because he's getting to get the heroes to stop being dicks to people, but there's something wrong. He tells me one day that he's going to find out and if he's not back, then to get the hell out of town. Instead, he comes back, but there's something funny about him. He doesn't remember anything about mom or me and sometimes he's just staring off. Sometimes he starts laughing for no reason. It's really weird. But at least he didn't stop me so I could at least get those lives. They came in handy."

Indira wondered if she should ask about these lives she kept referring to, but Esther was not shy about it. "Yes, I killed people for those lives."

That had not been what she was expecting to hear, but Indira knew she probably shouldn't have been surprised. After Esther told her who her mother was, she had looked up Lady Godiva, career assassin that had a brief stint in the villain game. There was next to nothing about her abilities except for a few rumours that she would never die, though Indira didn't know what that meant. Until possibly right now. "Is that hereditary?"

Esther nodded. "If dad weren't here, I'd have probably let everyone think I was dead and made a break for it." A look crossed her face like she was considering it more and she shrugged. "And if I left, I'd never find out what was in that room that drove them nuts or find out how any of this stuff works." Her eyes sparkled conspiratorially and she looked to Indira, daring her to ask and debating how long she was going to make her wait before she told her everything that was in there.

Indira was willing to take the bait. "You say that like you looked into the room."

"It's just people," she said. "They keep people in these rows of pods across the room, but they have the sections kind of separated. They brought me back in there after they killed me off and raised me. I think they didn't realize what was going on because I came back whole. That was what they called it. Whole. Apparently they usually only try to keep the people who are just barely hanging on and don't really have much going on upstairs anymore. But I saw them putting Penny into one of them and she wasn't looking too good already."

Indira made no move to stop her or ask anything further. She didn't need to know that Penny was suffering. She had Matt already telling her that. She could only hope that her mind was still working.

"I wasn't wandering around for that long," Esther warned her. "I surprised them by having my head together and they killed me again. And someone put me in the ground, which was a pain in the ass to get out of by the way. But they're doing something in there. It's a bit of a mess. They've got a list running of people that they're planning to track down. You should probably warn Matt, Brittany and Laura, by the way. I don't know what it is—"

"They're planning to extend the program," Indira told her, making a note to call Matt and the other two back. She'd left on such a bad note that she was now looking around for her phone. She'd thrown it around here somewhere.

"Oh god, really?" Esther asked, watching as Indira started checking under her bed for her phone. "They have a list of people they're looking to round up for it. There's some big tech project they need to get done first and there was something about figuring out how to make a second core? They need it for broadcasting and some other stuff. Probably the whole zombie thing. It looked like they were working on alternatives if they couldn't figure out a way to duplicate whoever they have at the core. I never saw who it was, but it sounded like something was going wrong with them."

"A part of that core broke off and left me in the middle of nowhere," Indira told her. "And she's in half my classes now, too. Long story. Thanks for helping me get back, by the way. I wasn't sure I was ever going to find my way back after that."

"Thanks for not throwing up on me," Esther said, smiling as Indira finally found her phone by her nightstand. She held down the power button to turn it on. "Say, does your dad happen to have any psychic powers like you or whatever it is your brother can do? I'm assuming he can do something."

"Dad is literally the only person in this house who doesn't have any powers."

Esther looked hesitant before she nodded and Indira knew there was bad news on the way. "You might want to warn him, then, because he's on the list of people to possibly replace the core. They might have thought that, since your house had gone off the surveillance grid, he could do something. And I mean, technically, there is *someone* in here who could probably take over for that core, but it's not him, right?"

"I'm not as strong as she is, if that's what you're getting at," Indira told her.

"But you might be enough. They just need a psychic powerful enough to link a bunch of people together and make them do what they want them to do. And I know you're still keeping some of your cards hidden, but I'm pretty sure that if whatever they're trying doesn't work, you're going to have to watch your back. Because they're going to find out real quick that your dad isn't going to fit."

"We moved here so he'd stop getting kidnapped," Indira muttered, though she let the subject drop. The light on her phone flashed, trying to draw her attention. She had a lot of missed calls and texts, which didn't surprise her. She'd been quick to vanish that day. That day being Wednesday. And it was now five in the morning on Sunday.

"That dick," Indira muttered, gripping her phone and resisting the urge to throw it again. She had to let Matt know that she was okay. She tried to reach out to his mind, but her head started to spin as soon as she tried. She stumbled on her feet, Esther catching her and helping her back to sit on the bed.

"Ugh," Indira groaned, one hand running through her hair. "I don't think I'm that good yet."

"What were you doing?" Esther asked.

Indira felt nauseous and lowered her head between her knees, her eyes closed as she waited for it to pass. "Matt," she told her, offering her phone. "I figure leaving like that, hanging up on him, then going missing for three days is why I've got that many missed messages from him."

"He does look pretty worried," Esther agreed as she scrolled through the messages. "I got this." She walked out of Indira's line of sight to the corner of the room and called him before Indira could utter a protest. Indira didn't dare even raise her head, her body threatening throw up once again if she tried to move.

"Hey, get your ass over here," Esther snapped into the phone. "*Priorities*, Matt. Yes, I know what time it is. Do I sound like I give a shit? They're not going to be watching you right now, so just pop over."

Esther hung up and tossed the phone back down by Indira's side, her own butt following soon after to sit next to her on the bed. Indira felt her hand on her back and felt a little better about life, though her world was still rocking uncomfortably. She had never been gone this long and was feeling the effects. She was weaker than she thought she would be. Her stomach turned again, this time alerting her to just how long it had been since she had a meal.

"Matt should be here soon," Esther said. "You going to make it?"

"I need a sandwich," Indira said.

CHAPTER 12

INVENTORY

DESPITE THE UNFAMILIAR kitchen, Esther managed to scrounge together everything she needed for a sandwich. Indira waited with her head down on the cool counter as Esther busied herself making it, occasionally asking where one thing or another was while making far less noise than someone should in a kitchen. It was fine by Indira, who managed to find herself some aspirin on the way downstairs and was waiting for it to kick in.

She heard the plate slide in front of her and looked up, finding a tower of food between bread. Her stomach grumbled in approval, distracting her from the new buzzing echoing at the edge of her mind. "Thanks. Can you get the door?"

Esther went for the door and Indira started in on her sandwich. She didn't realize just how hungry she was until that first bite, but three days of her body in a psychic stasis had her ravenous. Every bite helped make the world a little more steady and dull the buzzing in her head subsided a little more.

The door opened before the knock came, Indira catching sight of Matt out of the corner of her eye. He stopped in the door, eyes locked on Esther. His jaw hung open, words on his lips that never made it out. His thoughts were frantic and piling on top of one another, but none of them would rise to the top as more kept piling on. He was only getting louder as Esther pulled him into the house and closed the door.

"Matt, can you please not think so loud right now?" Indira asked from the kitchen.

"You're alive," he said, following Esther into the kitchen. "You... How are you still alive?"

"Miss me?" Esther asked cheerily.

The cacophony of Matt's thoughts gave way to clarity and he closed the distance between himself and Esther, scooping her up in a hug. Esther let out a laugh and let him, wrapping her arms around him and giving him a squeeze before he let her go. His joy tapered off as another thought entered his mind and he looked wildly around the room. The walls had been painted to cover the specks, but he knew they must still be there watching them. "Are we going to... are we clear?"

"We're safe," Esther told him. "Whole house is. Apparently Shiraz whipped something up to stop anything listening in on the room or something." She gave him a playful smack on the arm. "And you didn't get your ass caught trying to get your sister back somehow. I'm impressed."

"It's not like I haven't wanted to," he said. "But it's been taking me a little longer than expected to get over last time. Not to mention someone's been trying to talk me out of it. Speaking of, is she…?"

"She'll be fine," Indira said, wiping her mouth of whatever she had gotten on it and squeezing her eyes shut. The world hadn't quite stopped yet, but she would be fine. Eyes open again, she relaxed and looked over at him. "She just needs to remember to lay off the powers for a little while until her brain comes all the way back together."

"What happened to you?" Matt asked. "You didn't sound so good and then you just didn't show up at school on Thursday. And you were absent on Friday. We thought something had happened to you."

"Oh, something did," Indira said. "The specks got Shiraz. They'd already cleaned the place up when I got here, but Mom got him out of town just in time, apparently. He wasn't looking too good, but he should be okay. Mom would have known if something was going to happen if he didn't. Although, I guess she did know… I don't know. I'll try to get in touch with them when it's daylight."

"That doesn't sound like it would take that long," Esther said, sitting down on one side of her at the island. Matt took a seat on the other, his eyes still trailing to Esther as if she were going to disappear at any moment. "And I hope your brother's okay, don't get me wrong. But I'm thinking you wouldn't be stuck unconscious like that for that long if you were just trying to make sure he wasn't dying."

"I also went to see if I could get into the white room," Indira admitted. "Not the smartest thing I've ever done, I know, but I haven't been back there since the last time. And it's not as strong as it used to be, so I figured I'd be okay. And I was for a while. That presence, Iris, isn't really paying attention like it used to be and I got right up to the edge of it. I was doing good for a while, until I got stuck again."

Indira immediately held up her hand to stop their protests and concerns and scolding about how she should have known better. "I got lucky," she said, slowly and loud enough that they understood her. "Estelle was there and she pulled me out of there."

"Who's Estelle?" Esther asked with a frown. "You couldn't have at least found a chick with a different enough sounding name to replace me when you thought I was dead?"

"I'm pretty sure you were actually dead," Matt told her. As happy as he was that she was alive, he still wanted to know why.

"Oh, I was," Esther assured him, reaching over Indira to pat him on the head. "I got better. Just like every other time."

"Other time?"

"So Estelle?"

"Estelle isn't replacing you," Indira said, knocking her shoulder into Esther's playfully. "She's new at school and she hasn't actually shown up yet. She's this projection, but she's tangible. It's weird. Powerful stuff, but she's the one that pulled me out of there. So get this," Indira said, turning back to include Matt in the conversation again. "Estelle is basically that white room, but she managed to split some of herself out of there. Apparently she doesn't like it in there either, and now she's got a crazy idea on how to take it all down. She's on our side, but her idea is just dumb. But in order to get it rolling, she decided she needed me out of the way for a while, so she stranded me in the middle of nowhere for the past few days. I've been trying to get back. I almost didn't. I couldn't find my body anywhere."

"You mean you've been asleep like that since Wednesday?" Esther asked. "No wonder Kyle looked so pissed."

Indira turned slowly to look at her. "What do you mean *Kyle* looked pissed?" she asked.

"So, I've been watching your house since yesterday," Esther admitted, not meeting her eyes. "I saw Kyle come by with some chick who looked like she could be his sister and she went off somewhere, but he just walked in here looking like he was ready to start a fight or something. Your door was unlocked, by the way. He was only inside for about five minutes yelling for you before he rushed out and looked like he had some kind of renewed purpose in life or something. And that's when I slipped in." Esther turned to Matt. "Figured I'd lock the door and grab a bite to eat before I found sleeping beauty here completely unresponsive."

Indira let out a long, irritated groan and buried her face in her hands. "Estelle," she said, her hands dragging down along her face and she let out another grunt of frustration. "That's probably who you saw. She's got it in her head that if she can convince Kyle to become a superhero, he can take down his father. She's like a second Kyle if Kyle were trapped and forcing people to sustain this weird little city forever."

"If I didn't know better, I'd think you didn't like Whitten," Esther said. "It sounds like Estelle has literally never met Chief Hollins and has no idea what she's up against. Kyle's going to be dead before Hollins even knows that he's left the house. Hell, he might be dead before he leaves the house. He sets the specks off constantly as it is."

"It's worse than that. Estelle and Iris are both Aunt Tess."

Esther gave her a look and Indira knew what was coming. Esther dropped down from the stool, landing hard on the ground and threw her hands up in the air. *"I left the city to get away from this shit!"* she yelled. "Does this convoluted bullshit have to keep happening *everywhere?* Just once, can't someone want to be a bitch because he's got a tiny dick or something? I swear to god, I'm going to cut every asshole I can find in this town."

"Does this happen a lot?" Matt asked, looking amused.

"Way more often than you'd think with big time hero and villain stuff," Indira said, both of them watching Esther as she gestured and continued to rant back and forth into the living room. "Especially the villain side of things."

"You okay?" Matt asked as Esther started to quiet down again. "Or do you need another hour?"

"I am going to need a lot longer than an hour," Esther said, shaking her head and still obviously irritated. "Let's change the subject. You said they shot your brother? Can he even do anything? I mean, I kind of figured you were the only one in your family until earlier, but what did he do to get his ass shot? I mean, if he's building stuff to knock out the specks but he's not magicking them up, why are they shooting him?"

"Raz just knows when people are going to die," Indira said. "He was working on something before he got caught. He kept saying the words to turn the specks on. I should really go back and take another look…"

Her eyes drifted to the stairs, but she hesitated before she got up. It was less being on her feet and more knowing what she would find there and whether or not she wanted others to see it as well. Next to her, Matt got to his feet and gestured her along. Esther went ahead, Indira trailing between the pair of them up the stairs. Esther opened the door, letting Indira in first.

"It looks like nothing happened," Esther said as she turned on the light.

Indira went to the desk and undid the latch. She took in a deep breath and lifted the top of it open, revealing the contents on the inside. It wasn't as bad as it had been when the blood was fresh and burning, but it was still pungent dry and she would need to leave it open to air it out a little if she was ever going to be able to deal with the smell of it. The look of it still left her feeling fragile and worrying that it was too much for him to leave behind and still survive.

"That doesn't look good," Esther said behind her, coming around to get a better look at the scene. "I'm guessing he knew to clean that up and close it before anyone got here. Surprising they didn't find it and check it, though. Are you okay? You're looking pale."

"I'm fine," Indira insisted. She reached forward, but her hand shook. She pulled it back, though she knew both Matt and Esther had seen. "That must have been what he was working on. He said that he didn't turn it on all the way."

Esther reached over and picked it up, gently wiping at some of the dried blood as she inspected it. There was a switch on the side that looked like it hadn't been fully moved into position, though so many wires were still loose. She clicked it all the way and it hummed to life in her hand, so mild that if not for her reaction, Indira wouldn't have known it was on at all.

"What do you think it does?" Matt asked. He went to sit on Shiraz's bed and Indira followed, standing beside him and away from the blood. Esther watched Indira for a moment before she fiddled with the latch and the desk dropped shut with a clang.

"He was working mostly on making the specks not work," Indira said. "He said when his desk was closed they couldn't listen. I'm guessing this thing also does something like that. It's small enough that I can guess it was supposed to be a portable version of it so that we could talk anywhere? And you said they were watching the house, right? Maybe they were trying to figure out how we were off their grid and they found him making this. He said he was testing it, which means he would have been setting off the sensors like crazy to do it."

"Your brother is as reckless as you are," Esther said, hesitating. "Can I keep this?" she asked, looking down at it. "It's going to be better if nobody finds out I'm back. Not them, anyway."

"If you can figure out if it's working," Indira told her.

"They're watching the house?" Matt asked, concern flaring in him again. "And me showing up here at six in the damn morning isn't going to raise a red flag?"

Esther fiddled with the device as she went to the window. Gingerly, she moved one of the blinds and peered out, a frown on her face. "Not there right now. You're good. They'll be back in about three hours, though, and eight or nine isn't a weird time for you to pop by."

"On a Sunday?"

"You?"

Matt and Esther stared at each other for a long moment, eyes narrowed in contention. Finally, Matt relaxed and shook his head. "Fine, not weird," he conceded. "Give me a break, all the women in my life are coming back from the dead. Next, Penny and Mom are going to randomly show up for breakfast."

"Don't get too used to me," Esther said. She pocketed the device without turning it off and patted it. "Now that you're alive again, I'm going to take this thing for a spin while I take care of a few things. I'll see what I can do about stopping in on you guys tomorrow, but I'm only a shout away if you need me. And it sounds like you are *definitely* going to need me."

The thought of Esther leaving after being told that her house was being watched left Indira feeling uncomfortable. People had managed to get in through the front door while she was away from her body. She didn't want to be here on her own. "Where are you even going? I thought your place wasn't an option right now."

"She's got places," Matt told her. "Be careful and keep in touch."

Esther smiled and opened the window. She slipped out and jumped down from the roof. Indira closed it after her, watching her disappear into the early morning. Her hands were still shaking and she still felt weak, which did not help her unease. She looked up and down the street for anything unusual, but it looked like it always did. The cars were the same as usual, even at six in the morning. "I should have asked what to look for," she muttered.

"You don't look so good," Matt said. He was at her side, lowering the blinds again.

"I'll be okay," she said. "I've been out for days. It takes a bit to get back to normal." She didn't mention that she'd never been out for this long before, or that she wasn't really sure how she was supposed to recover. Her stomach gurgled loudly. "I think I just need a little more food."

"And some company?" Matt smiled and Indira was almost certain it wasn't a request. He followed her down to the kitchen and ushered her into a seat, going through her fridge to find leftover rice to microwave. She was grateful for the company, and for the fact that he wasn't pressing for information.

Indira nodded around the rice. The house might be safe on the inside to say and do whatever she wanted so long as Shiraz's desk stayed closed, but with people possibly outside watching, she didn't want to be in here all day. Her father was away on a project, her mother and brother in Vancouver, and there were not nearly enough places to hide in here if anything decided to break in on her. It would look strange if she abandoned it entirely, but she didn't want to be here alone for too long. "Stick around for a bit?" she asked. "I don't really…"

She didn't have to finish the words. Matt understood, and he had no intention of leaving her alone right now anyway. He smiled and dropped down into the seat next to her once more. "Wouldn't dream of it," he said. "You want to hear about what you missed since you ran out on us?"

CHAPTER 13

CLEARING HEADS

MONDAY MORNING GREETED Indira with missed home-work, as well as a series of questions from various teachers on her whereabouts the past couple days and just where her brother was. Indira gave them her father's number at work so they had a parent who was in town to speak with, and gently suggested they ignore the fact that she had been missing for a few days.

Her attempts to get in touch with Kyle on Sunday were fruit-less, so Indira hoped that he would be there in the Welcoming Committee room that morning. There were plenty of faces that turned to look at her in various states of alarm and relief, but Kyle was not among them. Indira frowned, but reminded her-self that they had first period together. She would see him soon enough.

"I thought you were dead," Damien said, looking around the room reflexively to see just who could hear him. He was pouring over something with Brittany while Ronnie was working with another new student, a girl who'd actually decided to take them up on tutoring. Indira could tell from how Damien was mentally shouting at her that she was not among the powered students, though he still had plenty of other things he wanted to ask. They all did. She glanced up, noting that the device Shiraz had installed looked like it was still working, though she kept her words confined to their heads for now.

I'm fine, she told them, letting Brittany and Ronnie hear her as well. *But we're going to need to talk. We're going to be moving sooner than later.*

Good, Brittany replied as she let her eyes wander back to the sheets in front of her. *I'm getting sick of waiting around and doing nothing.*

"So, what did I miss?" Indira asked out loud.

"I think that new girl is trying to move in on your boyfriend," Damien said. Brittany elbowed him hard and glared at him to shut up, which earned her an indignant look in response. "What? It's a dick move *not* to tell people about that kind of thing."

"I'll deal with that later," Indira said, leaning between them to see what they had been looking at. "You guys have a new student coming in this morning, right? You have it under control?"

"You seem really okay with this."

Indira smiled sweetly and patted him on the shoulder. "I got this," she said. "You just worry about making Genevieve feel welcome at Larkdale and you leave what my boyfriend and his new friend are doing up to me."

The first bell rang and Ronnie started to pack up with the new student. Her first class was across the school and she thanked him quickly before she ran out. Ronnie's class was several floors away, but he lingered behind to talk to Indira, the worry on him radiating as he packed up. She waited at his side and waited for him to finally ask her about her brother.

"Hey," he said nervously. His mind was working hard, like he was trying to remember why he was so worried.

"Shiraz'll be okay," Indira said, letting her shoulders drop. He was having trouble remembering already, and Shiraz wasn't even dead. "He got out of town with Mom. No one saw him dying, so he's probably going to make it. I'll get back in touch with him if I can, but it's a bit hard to reach him from in here. Whitten has a bit of a problem with anyone getting out of here with a signal, if you know what I mean." She shook her head and frowned at it. "But he's going to be fine."

"When you and him stopped showing up..."

"You remembered us," Indira reminded him. "When you don't remember us, then you have to worry, right?"

She smiled, though Ronnie took little comfort in it as he left. Indira followed soon after him, shaking her head and letting out a breath. It was a small comfort to know that they would be promptly forgotten if anything did happen, and he *had* started to forget Shiraz already. The worry lingered, which was good to know, though he was having so much trouble coming up with a name and face to match it to.

But there were other things she needed to concern herself with right now. It was first period and she was going to have to get this idea out of Kyle's head if she could. Matt offered to help keep Estelle away from him if he could manage, though it was going to be hard when she sat next to Kyle as often as she could.

Kyle was already in class sitting next to Estelle, both of them with their heads close together and discussing something in hushed tones. Indira put on a pleasant smile, one that she didn't feel in the least, and prepared herself as she approached. She put her hand on Kyle's back and the other on the back of Estelle's chair. "Hey," she said. "You're not answering your phone. Is something up?"

"Indira!" Kyle said, standing up to collect her in a tight hug. "You're…. you…"

The happiness quickly faded from his eyes, turning into confusion. Indira could see that Estelle had been busy feeding him the idea that she was dead. Standing here in front of him was very wrong to him. Indira glanced over his shoulder to see Estelle furious that she was back and offered her smile and a wink. She gave Kyle a tight squeeze to let him know she was real and took a peek at just how much of his mind he'd let Estelle pollute.

"Seriously, you've gotta check your phone," she assured him. "I've had people telling me some stuff and if I didn't know better, I'd be worried."

"You're okay?"

Indira narrowed her eyes at him like she was trying to decide if he was kidding. "It was a flu."

The second bell sounded, though their teacher had yet to materialize. Instead, Matt appeared at the desk, his eyes going between Indira and Kyle with a knowing smile. "Hey, apparently we've got a sub today," he said. "You wanna switch seats?"

"He better," Indira said, giving him a warning look. She tugged him to the back of the room, leaving Matt to deal with Estelle before she could think of anything. He was quick to start talking to her, keeping his tone light and pleasant and his mind closed while Indira got Kyle out of the way. The distance wouldn't do much to keep Estelle's influence off of Kyle, she knew, but it might make it easier for Indira to keep him focused.

"All right, if you'd all sit down," a man said from the front of the class. Their sub looked familiar, though Indira didn't think anything of it. Estelle reluctantly turned her attention to the front as class started, and Indira stopped paying attention entirely.

She leaned in close to Kyle. He pushed his open textbook over to her and she could still feel the confusion coming off of him. "What did I miss?" she asked. His mind was covered in little sticky white strands from Estelle, all trying to convince him that he was willing to do whatever Estelle wanted. They weren't as sticky as the ones that had been on Matt and Penny's minds before and didn't stick to Indira in the same way. They were less potent, though no less irritating to start picking off.

"Not much," Kyle said. "We finished the presentation. I think you're getting the grade even though you weren't here for it for the stuff you did. Where were you? I didn't hear from you for days. No one did. It was like you'd died or something. I could have sworn you'd..."

"I got sick," Indira said. "Stuck in bed and my phone was off. Sorry about that. I tried calling you yesterday, but you wouldn't pick up."

"I'm sorry," he said, sounding conflicted as she brushed more of the white stuff off his mind. It fell away like powder, no stickier than rice and easily flaking off, though she found roots digging in underneath those. "You were dead, though. Dad, he wouldn't let the heroes in so that they could save you."

"From a *flu?*" she asked him gingerly. "That's a little dramatic, don't you think? I'm pretty sure I don't need saving from a flu. Unless you were breaking into my house and watching me sleep while I was sick. Because then I might need someone to save me from my creepy stalker boyfriend. But you would never do anything like that, would you, Kyle?"

"Oh, no!" he said, perhaps a little too loudly. He looked around, embarrassed as he lowered his voice back down to talk to her again. He was embarrassed about what he'd done too, though that memory of him standing over her bed and becoming convinced that he had to find a way to save her was muddied and shifting, even now.

Indira laughed softly and leaned into him. "I know," she said. "I'm sorry I disappeared on you, though. Make it up this weekend? We haven't had a chance to go out in a while and it's a short week."

"Friday?" he asked. "Uh, my mom said she wanted to have you by again. I've been trying to talk her out of it, but she's really insisting. And I think dad's going to be at work all day on Friday, so you won't have to deal with him. I'm still really sorry about him. I really need to do something about him. Stop him or—"

Indira put her hand on his arm as she saw Estelle trying to get into his head again. She guarded his mind, putting up a shield to keep her out, though Estelle had already left her mark inside. "Friday sounds good," she said, trying to think of a way to get Estelle out of his head completely.

They sat through the rest of class, quietly talking amidst the silent reading. Every instant that Indira let her attention drop, Estelle would make another jab at Kyle's mind for Indira to deal with, though she was leaving behind more and more marks. It wasn't difficult to find a way to give Kyle a reason to be angry at his father about heroes, after all. He did that fine on his own. The thing Estelle was doing was only coaxing that anger in him and that was what was making it so infuriating to deal with. It was because she wasn't poisoning his mind so much as she was encouraging him to continue his thinking to a dangerous conclusion.

As class finally wound to a close, Indira and Kyle smiling and chatting quietly at the back of the room, Indira knew she had to do something to keep Estelle out of Kyle's head. She could shield him for now, but it wouldn't last forever. Estelle's ideas were going to get him killed. On top of that, the fact that Indira was not dead yet was not getting through to him. When he looked away from her too long, he seemed to forget that she wasn't still lying in bed, completely unresponsive. It was becoming clear that she was going to have to go through Estelle to keep her from trying to use him as a pawn in this.

"So Friday?" he asked, smiling as he stood. "I mean, before too, but we're on for Friday? I can tell my mom?"

The class was filing out past them, but Indira was paying more attention to the one person keeping an eye on them. She reached up and cupped his chin, pulling him over to her and their lips met. It felt like a while since they kissed and Kyle seemed to know it, given how eager he was. Indira took the moment to push back into his mind, sending the white bits that were Estelle away while encasing it in her own protection. The shield should hold for a little while, though she'd have to renew it before too long.

When Kyle pulled back, he had a goofy grin on his face as he looked around. "What was that for?" he asked, trying to figure out if anyone else had seen them and not sure if he was okay with that.

"It's been a while," Indira said, leading the way out. "What, a girl can't kiss her boyfriend?"

As they walked out, she passed by Estelle, who stared at her like she intended to set her on fire with a glare. Indira welcomed the look, feeling much more comfortable now about letting Kyle head off to his own classes without her and without worrying if he was going to go off and don tights to do something stupid while she wasn't looking.

CHAPTER 14

FAIR WARNING

"Is it just me or are there a lot of subs this week?" Kyle asked, looking through the homework for the day. They had much less than usual this week, which no one was complaining about. A short week with minimal homework was never a bad thing, and Indira was trying to get as much of it done now so she could dedicate the whole weekend to figuring out what they were going to do.

I think there's a reason for that, Damien noted. *I definitely know the woman who subbed for my History class.*

"It's probably just the flu," Indira told him. "It knocked me out too for a while, remember?" She smiled as the confusion flickered across his face again. He could mostly remember she wasn't dead now, which was a relief, but she still needed to keep an eye on him. Estelle had backed off for now, though Indira knew that wouldn't last long. Instead, she had hauled him into the Welcoming Committee room as much as she could, hoping that Estelle wouldn't follow to a place where Indira had backup. And lately, it was usually a fairly full room.

English sub looked familiar too, Indira noted. *Do we need to give them a heads up too?*

Brittany scowled from the couch, shooting Indira a look before looking back down at her phone. There was something different about her and Laura, *Already have your hands full, don't you think? Let someone else handle it for now. You have other things to worry about.*

Do you mean the boyfriend or the suicide mission? Damien asked.

She means both, Laura said.

"You know, we have all weekend to finish this," Kyle said, putting his pencil down and stretching wide behind Indira. "We don't have to finish it all now."

"Do you really want to be doing this on the weekend? I thought we could catch a movie or something. Hang out a bit. We don't just have to do Friday, you know."

"It's only Wednesday. And besides, are you sure your parents aren't going to get... you know." That wasn't what he was concerned about, but it seemed like an easier way to get her to change her mind.

Is your dad home yet? Laura asked.

"It'll be fine. I got it."

That's a no, Matt said. Indira didn't think he was listening given how he looked like he was about to fall asleep. It looked like Penny was keeping him up and drawing on him again. *You know, you can always come by if you don't want to be home.*

Yeah, she can just go hang out with her boyfriend's bestie without him, Laura said, laughter punctuating her thoughts though her expression stayed very still behind her laptop. *For the record, my place is also an option.*

Thanks, but I'll be okay, Indira told them. *Dad stopped by yesterday to check in.*

I don't like it, Brittany said. *You of all people shouldn't be hanging out that close to Chief Hollins.*

It's the perfect alibi.

"If you're sure," Kyle said after a moment. It occurred to him that he might have said something wrong, but other concerns echoed in his head louder, though less concrete. He knew there was something about his father, that he would be home on the weekend and that they would have to make sure they weren't around when he was. He had trouble thinking of why, every thought of his father sparking an ire in him that did not waver. He knew that he was going to do something about him. "I was going to..."

"It'll be fun," she said, bumping her arm into his. "Unless you were planning on spending the weekend with Matt again..."

"No! No that's not—"

Indira laughed and Matt joined in, letting it be known that he was eavesdropping. Kyle flushed, shooting a glare at Matt before turning his eyes down to his homework.

"I suppose I can let him go for *one* weekend," Matt said. "Don't get used to it."

The smile growing on Indira's face died as soon as the door opened. Estelle peered in, looking uncertain of herself until she laid eyes on Indira and Kyle. She straightened up and walked in, oblivious to the looks from the rest of the room, and pranced across to the pair of them. She put her backpack down by the table. "Hey, I've been looking for you," she said to Kyle. "We need to do that project for French. You don't mind, right?"

Indira plastered a smile back on her face. "No problem," Indira said, not moving. She let her arm rest next to Kyle's strengthening the shield on his mind. She wasn't concerned about Estelle, not in here.

Is she transparent to anyone else? Damien asked as he watched her.

He was the only one who said anything as Estelle commandeered Kyle's attention to their project, Indira idly finishing her own homework next to them. Her attention was on Estelle, keeping her from doing anything else to Kyle's head. It was quickly evident that Indira's shield was not enough, Estelle managing to slip into his head again and again before Indira pushed her back out.

It wasn't difficult to do so much as requiring her constant attention. It was more like keeping her friend's cat from taking her food than an actual battle, annoyingly persistent and easily preventable if she could just give Indira a moment to put a stronger shield over him. It wasn't one of her stronger abilities, but it should be enough for now.

Indira, why is everyo-

Indira blinked and looked up, eyes darting around the room. Estelle was forgotten in an instant, Indira finding that there was no one left in there with them except for Damien, now slumped against the wall and out cold. She looked back to Kyle, but he had stopped moving and his mind was buzzing with Estelle's influence. Estelle's smile was gone when she met Indira's eyes.

"You need to stop," Estelle said. "I already have this handled."

It was too late to hide the fear on her face, but Indira took in a breath and calmed herself nonetheless. She didn't know what Estelle wanted, but she protected herself first. She could get Kyle free of her influence once she got rid of her. "You don't have this even a little handled," Indira told her, glancing at Kyle. She didn't know how much he could hear. "You have no idea how any of this actually works. You're idealistic and you don't understand how the real world works in terms of this stuff, Estelle."

"He can't hear anything," Estelle said. "I'm not stupid. I know how this works. And I have it under control. *I'm* the one who they're making do all of this, so I know better than anyone how everything works. You haven't even been here a year. I gave you the chance to just sleep and stay out of it. It would have been over in a week."

"You were going to take down the towers in a week?" Indira asked her. She wasn't sure if she believed that Kyle couldn't hear anything but she couldn't help herself. "You were going to dismantle the facility that you've been staying in after a week? You were going to deal with the fallout of what was going to happen after everyone realized that there are a lot of people dead now because of your brother and the chaos that was going to come from that after *a week?*"

"You're making it more complicated than it needs to be," Estelle told her. "If you take my brother out of the equation and convince him to shut down the program, then everything else will fall into place."

"You have literally never been in a city after a big thing like this happens, have you?" Indira asked. "It takes years. The only reason you don't see it is because something else comes up, then another thing, then another thing. You don't have time to actually put the new laws in place before they're tested again and again and again. They banned powers here and now no one knows what that cost them. But they will. They're going to know full well what's happened when they unhook you from that thing, Estelle. And when he shuts down the program, a lot more things are going to fall apart than you think."

"I know what I'm doing," Estelle told her. "And I'm going to warn you once. If you keep going against me, I can make things a lot worse for you. I can remove you from this town just like all the others. Thanks to my brother, I've gotten very good at it."

Indira felt something tug at her mind and she pushed Estelle away. She put her hands on the table and leaned in toward her. She was not afraid of her, no matter what she tried to do. "You aren't pulling me out again," Indira told her. "And you aren't making Kyle do anything. He's not involved. He doesn't *need* to be involved."

She jumped when Kyle moved next to her, standing and turning to face her. His face was blank, eyes unseeing as he grabbed her roughly by the shoulders and turned her to face him. His fingers dug into her arms hard enough to leave a mark, his short nails digging into her skin.

Any breath she had left in her lungs flew out of her as he threw her to the side of the room. Her heart pounded in her chest, her body collapsing against the wall and staring up at the pair of them. Kyle stood there, sightless and emotionless, and Estelle looked down at her like she was trying to decide what else she could do to her.

"You need to back off, Indira," Estelle said. "I can already make him do whatever I want. It's better if *he* thinks he's doing it, though. Will is more likely to listen to him that way. It has to be Kyle. Will won't listen to someone with powers, but he *will* listen to his son."

Something was pulling on her mind, but Indira couldn't think to do anything. Kyle was bending down to her again and she cowered away from him, terrified of what was coming next. It wasn't him, she knew. Estelle was the one controlling him, but that didn't stop his hands from getting closer.

She let out a squeak as he grabbed her again and started to haul her back to her feet. She didn't know what he was going to do, but she might not be around long enough to find out. That pull was getting stronger, Estelle trying to yank her out of her body. Indira was unable to concentrate past the sound of her heart pounding in her ears and the knowledge that she was about to suffer.

"Although a little tragedy never—"

Indira fell to the ground, Kyle collapsing next to her. She scrambled back and away, desperate to get as far from him and his reach as she could. Her breath caught in her throat and tears stung her eyes, scrambling away until she hit the wall. She wrapped her arms around herself, tucking in her legs, and watched Kyle for any sign of movement, hoping that her legs would let her run.

Estelle was nowhere in sight. No one was anywhere. Indira's mind was completely silent as apparently the whole world had vanished. Or maybe she was shaking so badly that she just couldn't hear anything.

The door opened next to her and she jumped. Esther was there a moment later, looking first to Kyle's unconscious form on the ground, then Damien in the same condition on the other side of the room. Her face was covered in confusion by the time she laid eyes on Indira huddled in the corner behind her and staring back at her.

"Something happened in here," Esther said.

Indira put her hand the door to keep her from closing it. She rose shakily to her feet and pulled her along with her. "I can't..." she started, but the words couldn't quite come out. She couldn't be in there, not right now. She had to get away. She *needed* to get away.

Esther seemed to get the hint and led the way down the hall, slipping into the women's washrooms, and she did something to the door behind them.

Indira went to the sinks, putting her hands on the counter and leaning over them to let her forehead rest against the cool mirror.

Breathe. She just needed to breathe. It was okay. She was out of there and she was safe. Nothing was going to happen to her. Estelle was gone, so Kyle wouldn't do anything more to her. He probably wouldn't even remember doing it by tomorrow.

"Are you okay?" Esther asked.

Gently, Indira nodded and pulled herself away from the mirror. She looked back at Esther, her hair wild once more and dressed in colours that would attract too much attention for her to be here covertly. Wasn't she trying to lay low? "I'm okay. What did… Did you do something?"

"I thought I heard something happening in there, so I tried out an old trick," she said. "It's stuck to the door. Knocks out all powers in six meter radius. Like, twenty feet? Should be good for about twenty minutes."

"That's why it's so quiet," Indira said. The silence in her mind made her uneasy, but she was safe from Estelle at least. "We're not going to be able to…"

Esther smiled and brought a small device out of the purse at her side and put it on the counter. It was the thing she had taken from Shiraz's room that night, though looking a bit more polished than the last time she'd seen it. "Your brother does some good work. Haven't had a single speck catch me yet, and I've been trying. I hope you don't mind, but I decided to pay him a visit and make sure I knew how to work this thing properly. He says hi, by the way. He's doing okay and they say he's going to make a complete recovery."

"You saw him?"

Esther nodded. "Your mom's nice. She wants to come back and get you out of here too, but they're not letting her out of the building right now. Apparently she's really good about making sure that they all know just what awful things are coming to them because she's going to do them all to them personally if they don't let her out of there and come rescue her daughter. I like her."

Indira smiled. "Good," she said, more to herself than anyone else. "So long as they aren't coming back. I'm guessing Raz told her everything?"

"And everyone else too," Esther told her. "They're sending in a few people to Whitten to find out if your brother's accurate, but they're holding off on a big move right now. They haven't had a single contact come in that they've heard from again so far, so they don't want to risk too many people. Your brother's trying to tell them what's happening, but until they get confirmation of what's going on, they don't want to keep sending people in just to have them go missing."

"Raz have any ideas about how to get a signal out?"

Esther hesitated. "He thinks we have to take out one of the towers."

"He say which tower?" Indira asked.

"Remember that first one you saw?" she asked. "The one with Quantum on Halloween? He figures if we can get rid of that one, half the heroes in Vancouver will come running."

CHAPTER 15

CAPTURE THE FLAG

PROMISES OF HELP waiting outside the city was enough to make people volunteer, but Indira didn't like it. It was only Thursday night and she didn't have enough time to plan or look ahead. They had already been severely outmatched and nearly killed once trying to take down this exact tower, and she wanted more time to plan out *something.* One night of poking around the tower didn't give her enough of a sense of what they were going to be up against.

Brittany had insisted and gotten the address easily out of Matt, so Indira didn't have much of a choice. He knew they were both anxious and regretted telling them anything at all. Without Shiraz, she couldn't tell if any of them would make it in the end.

Too soon, they were piling out of a car several blocks away under cover of night. Where Damien was more curious than anything, Matt and Alan were appropriately hesitant about the matter, though they both knew just what they were getting into. Ronnie came out of a desire to not be left behind while something bad happened again. Laura and Brittany were there as well, both far too eager to see how much damage they could do if they really tried. A lot, from what Indira could tell.

Indira left her body behind, brushing her hair on her bed, and watched as the two young women left their marks to weave a spell over the area, creating a shield for themselves and locking them all in the lot with the tower, as well as locking everyone else out. Once everyone was inside, they knocked the area just a little out of balance, sending it off reality just that little bit that would keep the specks from paying attention to them.

"You still here, Indira?" Brittany asked as the spell was set, looking around for the projection that Indira hesitated to actually make.

Still here, Indira said though she knew her voice must be faint. Not being physically inside of it made it harder to latch onto the location and on them, but she pressed herself into the space. She wished they wouldn't risk talking out loud, but she wasn't going to be able to swing a trick like in the underground facility again. *It's a bit hard to keep in here with you guys. I'll keep an eye on the perimeter and let you know when things start coming for you.*

"Sounds good," Brittany said. The magic users went to the tower while the rest lingered around the perimeter to keep an eye on anything coming for them. Alan waited a moment before he followed to the tower, becoming incorporeal and gliding up the side of it to perch at the top. It was clear he wasn't comfortable up there, hunching over as much as he could to avoid looking like the target he was and remaining translucent.

"Relax," Laura yelled up to him. "We got you. No one's seeing you."

"Easy for you to say," he shot back at them. "You aren't in the open."

"We'll give them something else to watch out for," Brittany offered. She smiled and promptly caught fire, Laura following her lead. They went to the base of the tower, creating a ring of flames at the base of it and frying the circuitry that ran up the length of the structure.

"You know, I can help with that," Damien said. "They didn't completely block me."

"We got this. You watch our backs."

Matt popped the trapdoor open easily and jumped down to the narrow room and servers stored below. There was barely enough room for even him, but he seemed unbothered as he got to work.

"Why even bother with that?" Brittany asked. "We take down the tower and we're done, right? We can melt this thing down right now."

It will just rebuild, Indira said. She was no expert in technology like her father and brother, but she at least knew what she was looking at when she checked out the tower last night. *The signal comes from down in there, and it's doing something weird. I'm betting if you look, everything you just fried is already trying to repair itself.*

"It's magic resistant too." It was more like a curse coming out of Laura's mouth, the girl glowering as she started working on melting down the existing tower. With Brittany, she melted down the bottom of it into strange little metal demons that fluttered around them, ignoring how it regenerated. They made the demons faster than it grew back, though only barely.

Indira spotted the white vans and didn't question what they were here for. The doors opened before they had stopped, men in hazmat suits sweeping out and toward the tower. *Heads up!* she called. *We have company!*

"Got it!" Laura called.

The first of them came to the barrier and bounced harmlessly off the edge of it, followed soon after by a second. They tried again and again to get in, mindless in their repetitive attempts, and made it no closer. Creeping through the barrier, the metal demons surrounded and swarmed the first two. Distracted, they turned their attention to the little monsters trying to rip them apart. The hazmat men fought back, the creatures exploding into molten metal and shrapnel when they were hit too hard.

Matt, how much longer with that door? Indira asked quickly. Alan leapt down from his perch to Ronnie's side and the two of them moved to the edge as the original two hazmat suits were joined by three more. The birds and the metal creatures went down as quickly as Laura and Brittany made them, Indira she could see the barrier between them start to waver with their attention so split.

Almost… Matt forced something in the underground room and something broke out across the field. The barrier went out and Matt was thrown back at the force. Laura and Brittany both fell to one knee, their fires extinguishing immediately and the tower rebuilding around them. The birds and metal creatures fell away completely and they righted themselves.

Brittany leaned over the trapdoor, furious. "The hell happened?"

Ronnie dropped out of the sky, landing in Alan's waiting arms. He got Ronnie on his feet and pulled him back to the tower as the hazmat suits approached.

"Powers are out," Alan told him.

Ronnie was still stunned as Alan pushed him to keep running. It took a moment for Ronnie to snap out of his daze and start running on his own, much slower than he should be moving. He looked back and saw the men in the tattered hazmat suits following behind them.

"Fall back!" Alan yelled to the rest of them. "Powers are out!"

"I don't know what I did!" Matt yelled from inside the hole. He was already frantically looking through the flashing lights, trying to backtrack and figure out what had done it.

Let me see, Indira said, pushing herself to appear beside him. The wires and flashing lights weren't as confusing as some of Shiraz's experiments. It was only that there were a lot of them, and Matt pointed out the last thing he did to give her an idea of where to start. Nothing looked familiar, though there was something else in here that felt off. No, not in here. Just a little above here.

Briefly, she touched her body, noting the hand that still pulled her brush through her hair. This was not good. "Matt, this switch," she told him, letting herself drift through the machinery to a very small room behind the mechanics.

It was less of a room and more of a place to put a pod very like those she had seen in the underground facility. Inside, there was a grown man laying frozen, his eyes open and staring into the darkness. She could hear Matt fiddling with the switch and Indira got to work, pulling more of her presence and her powers into the projection. Her hand went through the glass to touch the man. She let her power spread over him, blocking his nullification powers. It would buy them some time, but it wouldn't last for long.

Those above let out a cheer as their powers returned, getting back to protecting themselves. Matt managed to get the switch thrown and light flooded in, a second trapdoor opening above her to reveal the pod to those on the ground.

"Ronnie, I need you to get this thing out of here!" Indira called up to them.

Ronnie swept over and picked up the pod, Indira staying on it to keep the man inside from setting off his powers again. Ronnie only made it a short way before he realized he had no idea what the plan was. "Indira, what do I do with him?"

"Chuck him as far as you can," Indira told him.

Ronnie looked like he was going to drop him out of surprise. "That could kill him!"

"Drop him out of the way, then," Indira told him. "He's already dead anyway. Remember that breathing doesn't mean alive." She didn't have time to worry about Ronnie's disgust with the idea of killing someone who was not coming back and she had a lot of other backs to watch.

Though he was shaking, Ronnie resisted the urge to look at the body inside and flew the pod a few blocks away, leaving it on top of a building before returning. With their powers back, the hazmat suits should be no problem, but above ground they hesitated. Indira looked around, seeing the advancing men in suits that had been shredded enough that they could see the people underneath. She could hear something echoing in the air, something just a little too quiet to make out, though she could tell that the hazmat suits could hear it.

"The hell is going on?" Damien demanded. The weapon in his hand, some kind of gun that Indira wasn't familiar with, was pointed toward the sky. He wouldn't lower it, his eyes frozen on one of the suits. "Indira, there's a guy in there! *I saw him die!* What is going on?"

He wasn't fast enough to block the streak of light coming for him. He barely made it out of the way and bit back a cry of pain as his sleeve bloomed with red. Blood dripped down his arm and he struggled to keep hold of the gun.

"*Just hit them!*" Indira yelled back at him. "They're getting more instruction. I can't block it. You need to stop playing nice and kick their asses into the ground *now.*"

"They're *people*," Laura insisted. "It's not like they're zombies. They're still alive."

"They aren't," Indira said. "They're resurrected. Brain dead. They might be walking, but they aren't alive anymore. And — *GET DOWN!*"

Indira forced everyone to the ground as one of them popped, a wave of fire spreading out from one teenage girl. Indira knew her where none of the rest of them did. She had come to their school and wouldn't stop being a hero, even at the cost of her life. She'd felt her die. And she was going to feel the rest of them die pretty soon if they didn't get their heads out of their asses.

"Matt, destroy the damn server. I'm calling in backup. Fall back and make sure no one gets too close to him. You think you can handle that?"

"What the hell do you mean backup?" Brittany demanded as she followed in suit. The monsters returned to swarm the hazmat suits once more. Brittany and Laura resurrected the fire around the base and scattered their metal demons. Alan ghosted back within the circle while Ronnie flew over it, picking up Damien and bringing him back inside as well. They weren't safe, Indira soon saw, with two of the hazmat suits already starting to take flight. Worse, another van pulled up with more suits already piling out.

Laughter came through the air as one of the hazmat suits dropped out of the sky and crashed down into the ring of fire, Esther riding his back dressed in sleek black with her hair tightly bound behind her as she steered the suit into the ground. "I think she means me," Esther said as she jumped off the suit's back. "Though I was already on my way. I just got a little held up. Hey, you keep that fire up," Esther snapped at Laura and Brittany as she dove through the flames, daggers in hand and ready to start cutting people up.

"The hell is—"

"I may have forgotten to mention it," Indira said, "but Esther came back. She needed to take care of something else, but I figured you guys could deal with this on your own without her. It would have been a lot better if you had, really. Now we're risking showing too much of our hand too early."

"You don't get to keep shit like that from us!" Brittany yelled back at her.

"Not the time," Laura said, coaxing Brittany to calm down and keep helping her with the fire and the demons. While Esther worked on the outside of the flames where they couldn't see, a couple slipped in that Ronnie was quick to sucker punch back outside while Alan dealt with the first aid. Damien remained stubborn, gun on his good shoulder and shooting at any flames that didn't look quite right.

With Esther's help, they picked them off until there was only one remaining. Esther threw the last one down through the flames, using him as a shield to let her through. "I need to show you guys something so you don't make me do that on my own again," she said, sounding and looking exhausted as she bent down over the body. The man inside the suit didn't even stir. Esther turned his head to the side and pulled down the back of the suit enough so that they could see the spot between his shoulder blades. Resting there was a mark that both Brittany and Laura recognized instantly, though the others were clueless.

"Yeah," Esther said as the recognition dawned on Brittany and Laura. "This is a common seal used on people who are about to die that you put on to make zombies. And the demon girls should be very familiar with it, am I right?" she asked, looking between the two of them. "Should probably be able to sense it and everything. And now that you know, you're taking care of this last one for me."

Esther reached into her pocket and clicked a button on the device. The suit got up again, but this time Brittany and Laura didn't hesitate. Their arms cracked and changed into metal blades and they cut him down, ignoring the blood that sprayed back up at them. Their power flickered, absorbing the kill, though not nearly as much as they both probably should have felt it. They were comfortable with dark magic, but they had not resorted to blood so far.

"Got it!" Matt finally said, pulling himself out of the hole. Metal creaked and broke under his feet, vines overtaking the hole behind him and pulling whatever machinery was in there apart. Above them, the tower stopped growing back.

"Damien, take it down," Indira said.

Leaning on a shocked Alan, Damien switched one of the settings on his gun and pointed it upwards. Light erupted from the end and sent him back down to the ground, Alan barely managing to keep Damien from hitting his head on the dirt. Above them, the tower faded away until there was nothing left at all.

"Miss me?" Esther asked, keeping her voice light and expression calm.

Brittany was a mix of relieved and angry. "How the hell are you here?" she demanded.

"Yeah, everyone thought my mom didn't have any powers either," Esther said with a bit of a smile. "Comes in handy when you need to disappear for a little while and organize the rescue party that's going to be coming into town. And, you know, gives you a few interesting opportunities."

Laura was happier to see her, throwing her arms around Esther and hugging her tight. "You came back! How long have you been back? *Why* did you come back here?"

"Are you that new contact?" Damien asked. He held his arm close, gun discarded on the ground as he looked her over. A frown tugged at the corners of his mouth. "I heard something about Godiva's kid going in and out of town."

"One, I have a name," Esther said. "Two, you stole that gun from a dead man, so maybe you keep that look to yourself. Three, I think we're good. A signal should be able to make it out of town and once they get confirmation that we're screwed, they'll finally send in the cavalry."

"Everyone get home," Indira said. She visibly faded away and let her attention spread out, seeing three more white vans heading right for them. "Before we get caught. More are already on the way."

CHAPTER 16

LUNCH DATE

FRIDAY WAS LIKE a reward for Indira after the stress of the last week. Her father still hadn't come home from work, and Indira was acutely aware of just how empty the house was of late. She drove to Kyle's house and walked with him and his mother to the restaurant for a meal that Kristie had nothing to do with. The spring day was bright and Indira was pleasantly surprised that Kyle's father was indeed nowhere in sight.

Kristie was much calmer than she'd been at their last dinner, more relaxed and open, though that wasn't the strange thing about the conversation. Both Kristie and Kyle peppered the occasion with strange moments of realization, suddenly able to remember names of people who Indira had never heard of before.

"Will's been very busy since last night," Kristie told her as they walked back to their house. "Apparently they lost a whole tower and haven't been able to figure out where it's gone. Can you believe it? How do you take a whole radio tower with no one noticing?"

"At least it should keep him busy," Kyle said. He gave Indira's hand a reassuring squeeze.

Indira smiled at Kristie. "I'm sure it will turn up somewhere."

"Did you ever meet Esther, Indira?" she asked, the name springing into her mind like many other names before it, this time with a face Indira knew. "A shame what happened to her. Kyle dated her for a little while. What happened to her again, dear?"

"Got hit by a drunk," Kyle said, looking decidedly awkward about his mother talking about his ex with his new girlfriend. He looked to Indira, more to check and see how she reacted to it and hoping she wasn't mad about the mention of his ex than because he was worried about the discomfort of talking about a dead friend.

"I liked her," Indira said somberly.

"I've been remembering all these people lately," Kristie continued. "And I'm realizing I don't actually know what happened to a lot of them. There were a few women who've moved into Whitten over the years and I still see their families, but I don't know what happened to them. Like that friend of yours. The twins. Matt and Peggy?"

"Penny, Mom. And Penny's not around anymore either. She went off looking for her mom, I hear."

"Yes, they said Gertie ran off, but she wouldn't have done that," Kristie said, with the same conviction that Uncle Ness had given before. "Gertie wasn't that kind of woman. And she loved those kids. No matter what, she would have stayed around for them. Would have kicked that husband of hers out before she left. Something must have happened to her, but I can't think what. She was here one day and now she's just nowhere. It's like she disappeared. You'd think we'd be talking about her running away from her family for years, right? We're still talking about when Yvette did it and that was six years ago. With Gertie, though, it just happened and we forgot about it. It's so strange."

"Dad thought you were overreacting," Kyle said. Indira couldn't quite read his intent behind those words because he didn't know himself. He wanted her to stop bringing it up, but there was much more there that he was having trouble with. Namely, it was because he was starting to remember people who had gone missing as well and it was starting to scare him just how many of the names coming up were people he knew. He didn't know how to process it. Remembering how his mother and father argued about it wasn't helping him figure it out.

"Your father *always* thinks I'm overreacting," Kristie said bitterly. "That doesn't stop it from being strange. You don't just forget about people like that."

Indira stayed quiet. Over the course of lunch, they had come up with many names and people who had left town, but forgotten about them soon enough. Already, Esther was fading from Kristie's memory. It was only a passing curiosity, but it was more than she had been able to remember about anyone in a very long time. Indira wasn't sure what had changed that would let her remember it, unless the towers were doing more than she thought.

Kyle had more trouble with it. There were more names for him and those names lingered in the back of his mind, Kyle keeping them close when they returned along with the conviction that his father had been behind it. There had been an argument, she was sure, and he'd convinced himself that his father had something to do with everything wrong with Whitten, though he wasn't sure yet what was wrong with it. He wanted to know why and he wanted to do something about the information he had. It was dangerous thinking and it was going to get him in a lot of trouble if Indira wasn't careful.

She could see Estelle's handiwork at work, but there was little she could do about it right now. It would take time to unravel it, and by the time she did, they might already be saved. She hoped.

They got back in the house to find Chief Hollins sitting at the table in the kitchen, a sandwich in hand and furiously at work at his laptop. Indira got the sense of frustration and irritation off of him, a feeling that said much more than it should have. There was no protection on his mind today and he was not paying much attention to them when they came in. Kyle stiffened at seeing him, as did his mother, though Indira fought to remain calm. He liked her before and she could only hope that trend continued.

"Will, what are you doing home?" Kristie asked, going to make tea with the hope that her husband was only stopping in. "I thought you were going to be at work until late."

He grunted over the laptop and looked up, spotting Indira in the room as Kyle tried to usher back to the living room. "Hey," he called, stopping Kyle in his tracks. "Have you kids heard or seen anything unusual? Noticed anyone strange hanging around lately?"

"I don't think so, Mr. Hollins," Indira said when Kyle said nothing. "Why?"

"Your friends notice anyone missing lately?" he pressed.

Indira shook her head. "Why do you ask?" Next to her, Kyle desperately wanted to pull both of them directly out of the presence of his father and to the safety of his living room.

"We've been having a lot of people reporting missing kids all day today," he said. "All phone calls. I'm starting to wonder if it's just some kids trying to clog up the system. Not a single person actually showed up at the station to report anything, but we have to look into every single one of these cases anyway. These kids are making my job much more difficult than it needs to be and I'd like to know who they are."

"I don't know anything about it," Indira said.

"Shouldn't you be working on those bodies they found up by third?" Kyle snapped at him, pulling Indira away and behind him. "Or the missing radio tower? Why are you asking us about something you think is fake anyway? It's not like you're going to do anything about it."

Bodies? Indira definitely hadn't heard anyone mention anything about bodies anywhere, though she was very aware of the mess they had left behind. She had assumed those would be cleaned up well before anyone found anything.

"Do either of you know anything about—"

"Of course we don't know anything about it!" Kyle snapped back at him. Indira could feel the tension in him and she didn't do anything to calm him down. His mother also said nothing as she busied herself in the cabinets, continuing like it wasn't happening at all. "Why are you even here? It's not like you can bring all your files with you. You're always talking about how you'd rather be at the office anyway."

"Sometimes," he said, lowering his glasses and closing the lid of his laptop, "a man likes to spend a little time away from the office and with his family. Even if his family is spoiled and ungrateful. Although I'm sure all of this is doing wonderful things in regards to impressing your girlfriend, Kyle. Women love it when you pick fights with your father in front of them."

Indira was very aware of Chief Hollins' attention moving from his own son to her. She avoided his eyes, but knew that she looked exactly as nervous as she felt. She was amazed that the man wasn't smacking the hell out of Kyle for talking to him like that.

Kyle narrowed his eyes at his father, his body going rigid. "You've been awfully interested in Indira lately," Kyle said. "Why do you always want to know things about my girlfriend, dad?"

"Your mother can ask and I can't?"

"No."

Indira wanted to run, but stayed put and forced her body to stay calm, though her mind was racing. Chief Hollins had been asking about her, and it seemed that both Kyle and his mother thought it was strange this time. Neither of them knew why, thinking that he had a more impure interest in her, but Indira knew otherwise.

"I'm just worried about her," he said casually. "All these kids going missing recently and her father hasn't been home for a while. Mother and brother out of town. How long have you been living in that house on your own now, girl? It's still concerning that your parents would abandon you at home alone like that."

"You've been watching my house?" Indira asked. The words came out like she was surprised, but it was more surprising that he was willing to admit it here in front of his family. She thought Esther had been mistaken, or that they had left since, but apparently they were still there. "Is that legal?"

"I think that's enough, dear," Kristie said, setting tea down on a tray and walking around them to bring it to the living room. "Tea?" she asked brightly, desperately hoping that Indira would go along with it and just let her serve them. She didn't know what else to do to relieve the tension in the room.

"Thank you Mrs. Hollins," Indira said, nervously eyeing the door. "I think I should probably head home, though. I've got a lot of homework and a test on Monday." She hoped Kyle hadn't mentioned that she'd gotten all of her work for the weekend done long ago.

Kristie looked disappointed as she set down the tea in the living room, but she understood. She shot a look at her husband in the kitchen, who was now packing up his bags to head to the office. "It's all right, Indira," she said. "We'll do this another time."

Indira nodded and got her shoes on, Kyle following her out the door and walking her the few feet to her car. He was fuming and shaking his head, but Indira knew she couldn't look too upset. Not while she was still so close to Chief Hollins. She took a deep, steadying breath. "So, how long did you know your dad was keeping an eye on me?" she asked.

He shook his head. "I didn't know he was watching your house," he said, desperate for her to believe him. "I really didn't. He just kept asking about you, even before all this stuff happened. I didn't think it was that bad, but…" He hesitated. There was something in his head that he wanted to say, but something else came out instead. "Maybe you shouldn't come by anymore," he said finally.

"I wasn't really planning on it," Indira said. "I mean, your mom's nice, but I don't think I want to be around your dad at all."

"I mean you shouldn't probably be around me either," Kyle said. He wouldn't meet her eyes. It was clear that he didn't want to be doing this, but he thought this was the right thing to do. Indira felt the pain he was going through in saying it, but she had to agree with him. Part of her wanted to blame Estelle for literally putting ideas in his head, but it seemed there was a lot more happening that he hadn't been telling her about. "At least until… I don't know if my dad's ever *not* going to be weird about this. I mean, I don't want to. I really don't want to. But we're probably a bad idea right now."

The words hit harder than she thought they would. She knew it was for the best and she knew that he genuinely felt the same and didn't want to hurt her, but he was trying to protect her. The unfortunate thing was that she was going to be in trouble with or without him. Indira took a deep breath, but she could feel the tears welling up in her eyes as she nodded. She didn't trust herself to speak.

He reached around and held her at the door of her car, hidden from the house. He was also having a hard time with this, which wasn't making it any easier for her to deal with. Indira didn't know what else to do, but she found herself hoping the last moments with him would last just a little longer.

"Call Matt," he said quietly in her ear. "See if it's okay to stay with him until your dad gets back home. Or at least until mine stops watching your house. He'll watch out for you."

Indira nodded, though she knew that she'd never be allowed to do that. Her father would refuse any request for her to stay at a boy's house, any boy at all. Besides, she didn't want to spend her time with Matt while dealing with heartbreak. She wanted to be surrounded by other girls and ice cream and romantic comedies. And she couldn't even do that because there might still be work to do.

CHAPTER 17

TRAFFIC STOP

THE ROAD WOUND around until she was in an unfamiliar part of town and driving past a sign reading *Whitten High School*. She had never been by the other high school before, and didn't much care that she was looking at it now, her mind too clouded by panic and fear and sadness. The sadness, she decided, she would deal with first. Breaking up with Kyle should be the most devastating of everything that had happened today, and now that there was no one around that she knew to see her, she let the tears spill over.

She didn't know how long she drove, through it was long enough for the sadness to be overtaken with the frustration at being lost. She ignored the messages on her phone for now and used the GPS to help her find her way back home to deal with the next issue. The house was being watched, which meant that she needed to get out of there. Even if the cavalry was on its way — and she had no idea if it really was — she didn't want to stay in a place that was under observation.

She packed a bag, grabbing her brush on the bedside table just in case, and took a seat on her bed. Everything felt like it was crashing down and she needed a moment's reprieve. The tears were gone, but she was trembling and, though she wanted to be alone, she realized she had never been quite as alone as this before. Her house wasn't safe and her family was gone. She wasn't sure what she was supposed to do now.

There was actually only one message on her phone when she went to check it. There was something strange about Kyle's best friend texting to check up on her, but Matt was one of her closest friends as well. *Kyle said you broke up. Are you okay?*

There was no way she was putting what she wanted to say into a text. With her house being watched, she didn't know what else they were keeping track of. Despite her still feeling shaken, she let her mind reach out to Matt and prodded at him to let her in. He admitted her immediately. *Chief Hollins is apparently watching my house,* she told him. *I need to find somewhere else to stay. You think Laura will take me in?*

Matt didn't seem even a little surprised by the request and didn't press to find out anything more. *She will,* he said. *She doesn't offer unless she means it. Is she home?*

Indira added her computer to her bag and grabbed a purse to throw a few more things she might need over the next few days into. She didn't know how long she would be imposing on Laura, but she couldn't come back to her house until she was sure it wasn't being watched any longer. She needed to talk to her father and find out what was going on, but she could do that once she was some-where safer.

She said she was going out with Brittany and their moms to do some-thing, Indira told him. *I'll ask when they get back.*

Come here for now, Matt suggested. She caught the lingering end of that. He was worried about her given the breakup and every-thing else happening right now. She might not want to be alone, which was as nice a reason to offer to come by as any. *I got something worked out so no one can even find the house unless they're on the safe list. It's probably a bit safer while you wait.*

On my way, she told him. She just needed to last a little longer and maybe she could just collapse on Matt's couch for a few hours. Maybe she just needed a little time to regroup, to figure out what she was going to do and see if she could find out what was happen-ing with this rescue that might be on its way. If they could figure out how to deal with everything that Whitten had set up to prevent anything from helping them.

It felt like something was coming. Her father was gone, her mother and brother were inaccessible, and she was waiting for Es-ther to bring in a cavalry that might not even work to rescue them. She needed to get her head together and work out the next plans in case the cavalry failed.

She threw her stuffed backpack and purse into the car and pulled out of the driveway, making her way to Matt's place. She pushed the thoughts of Kyle out of her mind, telling herself that it was for the best and that she needed to not worry too much about it. She could probably still get those ideas out of his head, and if she couldn't risk getting close enough to him to do it, she might be able to get Damien to do something close enough for her. She needed to concentrate on the problems of right now, which meant not worrying about a boyfriend she no longer had. She hadn't even seen Estelle since Esther had gotten rid of her, so Kyle was no longer an issue. And with Estelle gone, Indira could focus her attention on other things.

Despite following every traffic law, she was soon followed by a siren and police lights. Indira pulled over and leaned across to pull out her license and registration so that they would be ready when she was asked for them. In her rear view, she saw Chief Hollins got out of the car and approach her window. Her heart dropped. He knocked on her window and Indira struggled to remain in control.

Indira opened it half way, looking at him as calmly as she could and waited for him to ask for her papers. "And where do you think you're going?" he asked.

"To see a friend," Indira said. She knew not to question a police officer further when he was asking you questions. She was very aware of just how little traffic and how few houses there were in this stretch, and she knew that was intentional. She wasn't about to test him, and she certainly wasn't going to do anything that might provoke him if she didn't have to. There was a malicious air about him and she couldn't read him as easily right now. She couldn't tell if that was because she was fighting back her own panic, or if he had done something to prevent her from getting a glimpse at his head.

"Not studying?" he asked. "I'm pretty sure that's what you told my wife and son before you left."

He could have been doing anything other than routinely stopping her for not breaking any laws. She was driving the limit and stopping at every stop sign. He had a missing tower and several missing persons to attend to. Logically, this should not be happening right now. But it was.

Indira didn't say anything. She would not give him a reason. Though he apparently didn't need a reason to watch her house. Her heart beat quickly in her chest and she had to work to keep looking at Chief Hollins rather than casting her gaze wildly around for any help that might be coming for her. She didn't know what was going on and his second officer was coming up to the car to see her as well. From her rear view, she could see it was Esther's father, Officer Nava, his mind equally hard to read.

"Step out of the vehicle for me," he said.

"May I ask why?" she asked. It was a risk, but she didn't want to get any closer to him.

He smiled, Indira able to make out the point of his canines. "We have reports that someone matching your description was near the scene of a crime. We'd like to take you in for some questions. If you didn't have anything to do with it, I'm sure you'll be let off without much incident. Nothing to worry about. Just routine."

Indira couldn't think through the panic. She should stay calm, she knew, and do what she needed to in order to keep the situation from escalating. She opened the door but left the keys in the ignition as she turned the car off. She stepped out of the vehicle and kept herself straight and out of the way. She stayed against the car, pressing her back against it and failing not to let the fear consume her. "What crime?" she asked. "I've been with your son and wife most of the morning. And I was just talking with a friend before heading over there. I don't know when I would have time."

A smile cracked across his face. He was enjoying this. "Heroism," he told her. "Not a lot of people named Indira in Whitten, and there were a lot of people calling your name when that radio tower went missing. Not very careful of you at all, was it? That's usually why the big guys use codenames."

Indira didn't know what made her do it, but her feet moved before she knew what she was doing. She tried to run, but Officer Nava grabbed her and slammed her down into the ground. There were no cars or houses around to watch what was happening. He grabbed her hands, putting her in handcuffs, and kept her pinned to the ground. She needed to get away. She was caught and she needed to warn the rest of them. She needed to do anything but lie here with her face pushed into the pavement.

"Funny how your house stayed off the grid when it was just you in it," Chief Hollins continued as she was brought up to her feet and walked to the police car. "We're going to have a lot to talk about."

Her mind finally hooked on something she could do as the police car door opened. Matt. She was heading there. He'd be expecting her. *Matt, I—*

Something struck her across the back of her head and she collapsed into a heap. One more smack to the head and she was unconscious, the rest of her message lost.

CHAPTER 18

RESISTING CAPTIVITY

THE THROBBING IN her head both woke her up and kept her from coming fully awake. It was unpleasant and soothing all at once, the regular, deep thrum pounding in her temples in a low rhythm that told her that nothing was well and, though she would not be permitted to sleep through it, she didn't necessarily have to open her eyes to face anything just yet.

Still, she let her eyes drift open and immediately decided it was a bad idea. She was lying on a hard bench in a cell of a very brightly lit room. Her father was there was well, sitting against metal bars that didn't look quite right. It looked like he had been there for days, his clothing disheveled and marked with stains; his shoulders slumped forward, though whether from defeat or fatigue she couldn't tell.

"Dad?" Indira asked. She tried to raise her head, but a swell of dizziness kept her down. Right, they had hit her in the head, and probably fairly hard. She rolled far enough to grip the edge of the bench and tried to sit up again. The world insisted on continuing to spin around her and she leaned back. Her head rested against the cool wall and she gazed up at the white ceiling, wondering if this was what a concussion felt like. "I thought you said you were at work. This doesn't look like a robotics lab."

"Indira." The word came in a breath of relief. He went to her side, not sure whether or not to touch her and hug her and let her know it was all right, so he sat in front of her and put his hands on her shoulders. "Are you okay? What did they do? What do they *think* you did?" he added at the end, spitting it like a curse rather than a question for her. He glared back out at the hall on the other side of the bars.

"I got pulled over," she said, her head rolling to one side to meet his eyes. It didn't stay there long, and her father let her go. It was hard to keep her head upright and she let it drop into her hand. She could feel the scratches on her cheek as it brushed against her palm and everything was still moving uncomfortably. "Where are we?" she asked. "How long have you been here?"

Her dad shook his head and rubbed his finger over her eyebrow, brushing the hair out of the way and cleaning off some of the dirt from her face. "They pulled me into the office to talk about the project and then I was in here," he said. "They said they knew I was telepathic and wouldn't believe me when I said I couldn't do anything. For days, they kept insisting that I was hiding it from them, until they finally believed me. Then they said that it was someone else in my house. And now they want me to make you tell them what you can do. What do they think you did?"

"I don't know," Indira said. She couldn't lie to her father, not when he sounded quite that lost. This was a man who had stayed strong and been kidnapped before. Now he didn't sound nearly as good as he did when he had come back from being a prisoner. "A lot of things, probably."

"You don't tell them anything," he told her, pulling her close. "And more important, you don't *do* anything. They bring other people in here and wait for them to try and break out. When they do things, they start screaming. It's the lights, I think. I've seen them before."

Indira nodded dully, finally raising her head to look at her father. He had a black eye and he sounded so tired, but he was all right. It was comforting to know and she threw her arms around him, welcoming the small comfort of that, though she noticed the red specks watching them. They were listening and they were ready to fire if she did the wrong thing in here. Or if he did.

"I'm sorry," she said. "It's my fault you're in here. I'll get you out somehow. Maybe if I do what they ask—"

"No," he said, his voice firm. "I don't trust what they want you for, Indira. These are the people who will ask for a ransom and kill you anyway once they get it. You don't do anything they ask you for."

"That's bad advice, Byram," came Officer Nava's voice from the bars. Indira looked over to find him there, waiting. She knew what he wanted and she could see the red lights all on in the cell. There were too many of them active at once. They hadn't said anything to set them off, but still they watched. "If the princess is awake, we'll be taking her now."

"No," her father said, standing up in front of her.

A smile flickered over officer Nava's face and he looked pointedly at the lights around them. "Does your dad know what those things are?" he asked Indira. "He know what they can do? He doesn't know, does he? But you know exactly what they're capable of. You know what they already did to your brother. And you know what they'll do to your father if you don't come quietly."

"What is he talking about?"

Indira took in a breath as she stood up. She felt like throwing up, but she would not show weakness. Not yet. "I'm coming," she said, giving her father an apologetic look. She went to the door, already sensing that her father was ready to jump Officer Nava at the first chance he got. "He doesn't know anything," she pleaded with the man. "He can't do anything. Just let him go."

"Oh, not if he's going to be this useful," Officer Nava said. He slid the door open just enough for Indira to slide through. Indira looked back to her dad and silently begged him to stay put. He stayed mercifully still. That was something, at least. She let Officer Nava put her back in handcuffs before being led away from her father. She listened and took some small comfort in the silence that followed. At least they weren't hurting him.

While she wanted to run as fast as she could away from there, they had her father. If she did something and ran, they might take it out on him. If she could run at all. That hadn't worked out so well the last time and she didn't even know where she was. The threat of being tackled lingered, quickly being replaced by the fear of that gun on his hip, though she couldn't let herself be afraid of those things right now. Something else. She had to do something else.

"Keep moving," Officer Nava told her. His hand was on his gun and, though she tried, Indira couldn't access his thoughts so that she could tell whether or not he was actually planning on using that on her. She couldn't hope to use her powers right now, between the pain in her body and the inability to concentrate, but she tried to make herself calm. She had to keep herself together. If she didn't, they were going to take it out on her father. Even if he told her not to give in...

They were always told to go along with whatever your kidnappers wanted. In school and in the training they gave to the families of heroes, they said the important thing was to keep everyone alive long enough for help to arrive. Unfortunately, she had no idea if help would ever show up. They had only taken down one of the towers. It gave them a chance to verify that Whitten needed the help, but she didn't know if it was enough to send people in to save them.

Indira stayed very quiet as Officer Nava shoved her into a plain room and sat her down in a chair. He locked the handcuffs to the table to make sure she didn't leave before he left her alone. Indira, for her part, did her best not to show how scared she was and how much she was trying to figure out a way to get out of there. As soon as she was alone, she let out a breath and lowered her head, arms resting on the table and hair covering her face.

She forced herself to breathe deep and keep from shaking. She couldn't let herself imagine what was coming for her. She had to think. There had to be *something* she could do to get herself out of there. She wasn't like Uncle Ness and able to throw people out of her way. She couldn't break out of the handcuffs and didn't even bother pulling on them to try. There had to be something she could do on her own to get out of there. Something that would save her father.

Except that her father was safe. Mostly. They couldn't do anything to him or they lost their only leverage on her. They learned that one too, and it was repeated until they were sick of hearing it. She wasn't sure if that was actually the case, but in dealing with Kyle's father so far, she thought he was the sort to not worry about the people who couldn't offer him something. She might be able to resist for a little while before they started to use him to make her do what they wanted.

She needed to call for help, but she didn't know where she was. It was somewhere, she was certain, but it was strangely not where she was expecting to be. As she let herself go and her mind wander in the attempts to calm down, she found that she wasn't, as she initially assumed, surrounded by the white that was Estelle's diluted psychic abilities, so twisted and channeled by the others. There was something of a psychic shield here to keep her in but, as she pressed on it, she found herself confident that she could get through it if she really tried. She would need to concentrate, but she should be able to get through to deliver a message to someone.

It occurred to her that she knew this shielding. It was the same they used in the powers test to see how strong psychics were. She'd largely been far away by the time she entered the room and never had to actually deal with it before, not like this.

The door opened and Indira took a breath before she looked up, her silver eyes meeting Chief Hollins' blue ones. He took a seat across from her and put his laptop down in front of him, his expression neutral as he regarded her. There was a shield around his mind again, one that she assumed was from his sister being forced to do it, and she was unable to see what was in there, much less try to use it to convince him to let her go. He looked calm and almost pleased with himself, letting their eye contact drag on for minutes as neither of them said anything. The need to run or look away built up in Indira, but she knew that wouldn't help.

"So," he said finally. "What do you do?"

Indira said nothing, unable to come up with the words. Did he want her to confess? Explain what her involvement in the disappearing tower was? He asked the question like he wanted to know what country he should be sending her back to and… and he asked what she did. What she *could* do? Her powers? She knew she couldn't tell him about those.

At her silence, he rose to his feet, walking around the room and out of her line of sight. Indira kept her eyes straight ahead, listening to every footstep as Chief Hollins paced around the room. She waited, knowing that he would tell her what she was doing here. He would enjoy making her panic and she needed to not let it show how much it was getting to her.

"I pulled your files," he said calmly. "It seems your family has a bit of a history. Brother with foresight. Mother with foresight. And *you* with some telepathy. Very mild ability, apparently, that was fading over time. Strange how in a family of psychics, only yours would fade. It's not something that happens very often at all, as I understand it. Not when there's a family history."

Indira stayed quiet. So he knew that her father had nothing to do with anything. She hoped that meant that her father was safe. Maybe her father didn't know too much yet and he could just be returned, unable to remember he had a daughter. She resisted the urge to plead for her dad's safety or to say anything at all, instead clenching her fists and driving her nails into her palms.

Chief Hollins opened the laptop and hit a few keys. "It makes me wonder what you're hiding," he said. "See, heroism is a very serious offense in Whitten. It's illegal to commit, but villainy is far worse. And destroying a tower, even as an accomplice, is destruction of government property. That would definitely be filed as villainy. And you're from Vancouver, so I'm sure you know what happens to people guilty of that."

A tone started playing in her mind instead of her ears, emitting at a frequency that made her flinch. Chief Hollins smiled, looking like he'd just caught her. "One of the earlier forms of the powers test," he said by way of explanation. "This was how they found out my sister was one of you. This method was outlawed a little while later. They thought it was cruel."

He turned up the frequency and Indira struggled to maintain her composure. She kept her eyes on his, boring into them and not letting herself look away. She couldn't think, but she needed to get out of there. Her body was frozen and her mind was rattling. She could barely even concentrate on what he was saying anymore, but she knew that she was in trouble. Soon there would be an offer, though, if she remembered these tactics properly from when her uncle told her. When they made the offer, they turned off the machine and that was when she was supposed to try and run.

He turned it up again, Indira feeling it spike through her as the world around her started flickering white and black. "Funny," he said. "Your file says you're losing your powers, but if that were true, you would barely feel this. This was meant to take down only the most powerful psychics back in the day. Shame they retired it. I'm finding it to be very useful, myself." He laughed and Indira felt herself start to crumble.

"But we're having a bit of a problem," he continued. "I believe I've mentioned that we're duplicating the program for a new city. As much as I'd like to, I cannot seem to use my sister again in the new city for the program. I can't even use her to maintain the system here for much longer. I've been looking for a new core for the system, one that's young and strong enough to duplicate. And if I'm right —" he turned up the settings enough that Indira collapsed forward, breaking eye contact as her head hit the desk "— you might work as a replacement. And if not, we have other uses for you."

He dialled it back down, but Indira was still shaking and trying to pull herself together. "The question is whether you'll come willingly or if we have to hurt your father to make you comply. Unfortunately, the process does involve some cooperation on your part. But now you know what we will do to you if you try to act against us. And you know what we'll do to your father if you try anything. You've seen the— What do you kids call them? The specks? We're ready to fire as soon as you try to deny us and, believe me, we have ways to keep him alive for a long time after the first shot. So? What will it be?"

The frequency lowered to nothing, though Indira had no idea how she was supposed to escape like this. She still felt like she might collapse. Her brain was slowly reforming and she was not completely together. Her body wouldn't stop shaking. The threat to her father was enough. She couldn't think of anything she could do but offer her compliance. Compliance or…

A plan came to her as she shook on the table. She let herself remain weak physically, her hands still trembling and making her chains rattle. "Okay," she said, her voice soft and unsteady. "I'll do whatever you want. Just don't hurt my dad. Please. He's got nothing to do with this."

Chief Hollins nodded, a smile creeping across his face. "Good," he said, coming over to uncuff her and haul her to her feet. She was unsteady and she couldn't help but waver as he roughly hauled her to the door and to Officer Nava. "Take her and get her ready," he said, shoving her at him. "I'll be there shortly."

Officer Nava grabbed her by the arm and dragged her forward as she let her body go more and more limp with every step. He grew quickly tired of it and shoved her ahead of him. Indira stumbled, leaning against the wall, her body ready to collapse.

Her mind was already much stronger now that she wasn't in the presence of that thing. Nothing rattled in her head, but she had to be careful. If it looked unintentional, maybe they would leave her father alone. If she just looked weak, then they would have no reason to do anything to him.

"Keep moving," Officer Nava grunted at her. He grabbed her by the shoulders and pushed her forward.

Indira fell forward and collapsed limply to the floor. To anyone watching, her body was too shaken and weak from her interrogation to be able to remain upright and conscious. Her face hit the ground and Officer Nava took his time picking her up again.

Before she hit the ground, Indira took her consciousness and her powers and made a break for it. She didn't look back, not wanting to see what they had in store for her. Instead, she took a run at the barrier and forced her way through it.

They had her body, but her mind was free. Indira didn't bother trying to make a note of where her body was. She had to warn everyone and find someone to come save her.

CHAPTER 19

WARNING

INDIRA DIDN'T DARE hang around long enough to find out what happened to her body. She was tempted to go back and see her father, but it was more important to get as far away from there as possible. It was an impulsive move and she had to hope it worked but, as she started to move away from the police station and into the city, she realized just how bad an idea this was.

She left her body behind and they were moving it. She might not be able to find her way back. Not that she wanted to be back, but it was still terrifying to think that she might not be able to return. Worse, she didn't have anyone who might be able to break in and find her again. Before she'd always been in her house, where people would eventually come and know how to wake her up. Now, she'd intentionally left and she had no idea where she was going to end up or when she would ever even have a chance to get back.

But she knew where she would be. They would bring her back to the white room where they had Estelle. And, if they ever managed to take that down, she would be able to get her body back.

Indira finally stopped in the middle of a street, letting the cars pass all around her, and tried to see just how much of herself she'd managed to take with her. She was completely separated from her body and it felt like she had been able to pull everything with her this time, including the vague sense of where people were.

She went for Matt first, but he was moving. That wasn't an issue on its own, but trying to follow a moving vehicle when you were only a projection took a lot more finesse than she had practiced. She had to wait for him to stop moving before she could actually latch onto him. She came up on the vehicle, pulled over on the side of the road near the edge of town. She went around the side to see Esther sitting in the driver's seat with Matt in the passenger side, looking stunned and like he didn't know what was happening. Indira recognized the car as her own.

"Why are you stopping?" he demanded.

"Because we aren't skipping town," Esther said. "We're calling the cavalry. I'm not leaving her behind like that and, once you realize what the hell is going on, you aren't going to want to either."

"Who are you talking about?" he demanded. "I don't even know what's going on! Weren't you dead?"

"Dammit, Matt, get your shit together!" She was getting frustrated and gripped the wheel of the unmoving car as she snapped around to look at him. She winced as she tried to remember what was happening herself, though she knew there was something wrong. "We can't *both* be forgetting everything. Whitten's getting to us."

"Maybe if we drive out a little further," he suggested. "Get out of range?"

Esther shook her head. "Once it's gone, it stays gone," she said, struggling. "The hazmat guys were coming after you. And then we stole a car and started driving. And you knew whose car it was. Whose car is this? Who leaves the keys in the ignition and abandons it in the middle of the street like that? Why were you out there near a car? This isn't your car."

Matt pulled out the pages he was sitting on, finding registration looking at him. "It's not mine, but they had their registration," he said, trying to piece it together as much as she was. "We know whoever owns this car. But I don't think just pulling over on the side of the road is the best place to figure it out."

"I think I can help," Indira said, her projection strong enough that she could be physically seen sitting in the backseat of the car. The pair of them jumped and Indira leaned forward between them. "This is *my* car and you guys need to not get too far or I'm not going to be able to tell you to get to Laura's and tell her and Brittany to get to some damn protection *now*."

"Indira!" Matt said. He was happy to see her, but his expression fell as he looked from her to the reflection in the rear view mirror where she was not. "You're not here. You were... weren't you sup-posed to come over? What happened?"

"Routine traffic stop gone wrong," Indira told him. "A little police brutality. And I can't go back to my body for a little while, but that's not important. You need to get Laura and Brittany and get them to safety. If they're coming after you, then they'll be go-ing after them and Ronnie and Alan too. Can you tap the clock real quick?"

Confused, Matt tapped on the clock on the dashboard, his eyes flickering around at the car. "What does that do?"

"Makes it so no one can hear us."

Esther's hand launched back to grab Indira, but it passed through the projection. She let out a frustrated breath and glared at her. "Forget that, *what do you mean you can't go back to your body?*" Esther demanded. "You— What the hell happened while I went back? I swear, every time I turn my back on this place, someone does some stupid shit and leaves me right back in the fucking dark! What the *hell* happened to you?"

She wasn't getting anywhere with these two and she was going to have to go warn Laura and Brittany on her own. Her attention split and a second Indira wandered away, fading into nothing as she left the car. Her audience stared at her, looking from her to where her duplicate had disappeared.

"So it hasn't been the greatest day," Indira said. With that hope-fully taken care of, she had time to talk. "Chief Hollins has been watching my house, for one. Broke up with Kyle and I'm still a bit upset about that. On my way to Matt's place, I got pulled over by the police and got arrested because they were listening to the radio tower thing on Wednesday and my name was said. Found out they have my father in custody and they made me agree to be their new core to save my dad. So I kind of fake passed out and just got out of there."

Esther threw her hands up and they hit the roof of the car. "I *told* you they were watching your place!"

"Holy crap, Indira," Matt said, looking back at her with a mix of sympathy and trying to figure out the best way to word his questions. "So they have you now? Doesn't that mean you're screwed and they're going to make you into the new core and we're all fucked? We can't let you just stay there."

"We aren't," Esther said. She turned the car back on and started driving, though she didn't know where she was going to go. "And not just because everyone's completely fucked if they have you. They aren't taking anyone else for this crap."

"They can't actually do much," Indira told them. "See, I'm not there. I'm here. And a little bit of me is talking to Laura and Brittany right now and they are really pissed on my behalf and looking to go in there to break me out. And now they're taking a nap, because that is a terrible idea." Indira shook her head and called the other half of her back. "That was fun. But like I was saying, all of me is here. All my powers, anyway. And my mind. They can't even brainwash me to make me do anything on that end. I'm completely vegetative."

"You can do that?" Esther asked. It worried her, and she didn't like how calm Indira was about it. "That doesn't sound all that safe. I've seen how hard it is for you to get back to your body, and I'm thinking that might have been on a good day. How are you planning on getting back? And if you do, you're going to be in a lot of trouble."

Indira shook her head. "I'm not going back," she said firmly. "So long as they think they broke me, they're going to be stuck with their best shot as a vegetable. They're going to need to try something to bring me back and force me to come along, but I don't see them coming up with anything that's going to make me want to rejoin them and their little party any time soon. Which means I'm Casper for the next little while for all intents and purposes."

"What was that you were saying about a cavalry?" Matt asked Esther as he and Esther exchanged very disapproving looks. "I hope they can do something about this because this is starting to sound bad."

Esther laughed. "Starting?" she asked, shaking her mess of hair and taking in a deep breath, turning on her phone. She started texting as she talked. "Cavalry believes what's going on, thinks they can help, and they have a plan. Your brother *hates* the plan," she said to Indira, looking up from the phone to check the road as she said it, "but it's the only plan they got that has any chance of working as near as anyone can figure. They want to work from the outside in and take all the towers out before they go after the core, but no one's really sure what they're actually up against with that."

"Except you," Indira pointed out. "You were down there for a bit, right? You saw what was actually in there."

Esther shook her head. "I don't understand what I saw. I saw pods and I saw something in the middle. And you keep saying the core is a person, but there wasn't a person there. It was just, like, this tube that looked like maybe there was a person in there under the wires, but I don't know. I don't even know what to do with that. Like, if you stab the face, do you kill it? But they've taken Aunt Tess out of there, so how the hell does it even work?"

"Aunt Te— *Kyle's* Aunt Tess?" Matt demanded. He gave up the protest almost immediately. "You know what, I can go with it. But we still have the problem that Aunt Tess is making a room full of magic do whatever she wants. If she realizes what's going on and tries to defend herself, there's no way anything is going to survive that much magic. She's basically invincible."

"Only if there's any of her left in there," Indira said, a thought suddenly occurring to her. They looked at her, but she didn't give them the moment to question it. "How long is it going to take them to get everything together to start taking down the towers?" she asked.

"What the hell stupid thing are you planning?" Esther asked over her phone. "Because if this turns out to be some suicide mission on anyone's part, I know you aren't handling that well."

"Just get them ready," Indira said. "I'm going to make a call. And if it goes well, we might have a plan."

"You can't even use a phone like that!"

Indira faded out of existence, a smile on her face and waving as she disappeared. She watched as both Matt and Esther reached back to try and grab her, both forgetting that she wasn't really corporeal. Indira didn't do anything to help their protests, her mind already set to the next spot she had to go and the next thing she had to do. They would get over it and they would get everything together, she hoped. All she had to do was create an opening.

She hadn't seen Estelle anywhere, but she knew where a banished projection would likely go to lick her wounds. She went away from where the people wandered and into the places where it was much easier to get turned around and lost. She knew where she was going this time so she should be all right for once. Of everything for her to be bad at, she couldn't keep herself from getting lost between reality and the collective subconscious, the mess of small universes made of dreams and false hopes that the psychics so often got lost among.

CHAPTER 20

VISITING ESTELLE

NO MATTER WHERE she turned, there was chaos up here. Everything was in reds and golds like it was on fire, but no idea stayed in place for long enough for Indira to tell what they were as she walked through them. People were still remembering people they had forgotten and trying hard to hold onto those memories, to figure out what happened. Those memories stretched as they faded away, intertwined with more mundane ponderings.

Something pulsed through it, strong and calling to her. Indira went through the collective subconscious of Whitten until she found a large white shell in the middle of the chaos. Tentatively, Indira reached out to touch it and a door appeared. It seemed Estelle was waiting for her.

Taking a deep breath and pushing back that feeling that she was walking into a trap, Indira opened the door and let herself in. Inside, she found Estelle had created a world for herself to ruin. All around her, a very nice city had been torn to ruins and thrown in every which direction. There was nothing but debris around her and Estelle sitting in the very middle of it all, curled up in a small ball and looking smaller than Indira had ever seen her. She was younger now, looking as young as Indira thought she must have been when she went into that coma.

"We need to talk, Tess," Indira said. She didn't know what made her use the nickname, feeling the panic rise in her and she forced it back down. She didn't approach past the outer layer of the rubble, not wanting to scare her. For this, she would need Estelle on her side and Indira had not done a particularly good job of making a good impression on her.

Estelle's head snapped up and she grew. She got older, back into her teens, and then shrank back down to the twelve year old that Indira had walked in on. "What do you want?" she muttered, looking miserable as she didn't raise her head back up from her knees. "You're just here to gloat about how much better you are than me, aren't you? It's not even fair. You're picking on a little kid, you know. It's not good to pick on kids. That's the kind of thing only *evil* people do."

"As I remember it, this kid managed to keep me out of my body for a few days and was very determined to get her nephew killed with her plan," Indira said, unable to keep the spite from her voice as she said it. She had to remind herself that Estelle was only a child. And she needed Estelle on her side. "You were doing some bad stuff, Tess, and you weren't really thinking about the consequences."

"It would have worked," she insisted. "It always works. You just need to make someone whose *family* talk to them. If he cares about Kyle, then my brother would stop and listen to him. And Kyle can't do anything, right? So he probably cares about him a lot more than me. That's why I could never get through to him. Because he hates people like me and that's why he's gone and made me do all this bad stuff to stop them."

"He doesn't care about Kyle that much," Indira told her gently. "And he has so much of it automated that he might never know that it was Kyle at all. You see these things?" she asked, creating a couple of the black specks in her hand and showing it to Estelle. She seemed to recognize them, though she wasn't really sure what she was looking at as she crept forward. She stared at them and beckoned them over. Indira knew what she was trying to do and let her take the specks from her hands and look at them closer.

"These are the eyes, right?" Estelle asked, looking them over. "My brother spent a long time taking one of these apart once. He used to talk to me back then. He was so happy that he finally found the perfect place and thought it was like an Easter egg. I never knew what he made them do, but he said he could make them do whatever he wanted them to do if he was careful about it. And then he made a bug. And the bug went everywhere. And then the eyes started to listen and watch things. But they weren't dangerous."

Around them, Estelle's understanding of what they were came to life. The specks were around the city, watching people and making sure they didn't get into trouble. They were innocuous and not malicious. She thought little of them, probably nothing at all. "I helped," she said. "I thought he'd like me better if I helped. I'd turn the ones that got stuck and move them sometimes into better places so they could watch and make sure no one was doing anything bad. But then he started using them to find people like me. People with powers. And by then, I couldn't stop helping him anymore. But they didn't do anything bad."

"They do now," Indira said. She changed the scene, making someone in the park take off in flight. That person was shot out of the sky a moment later, then another person tried to run away too quickly. They were shot in the legs and then the back. "He has done a lot more tinkering since then."

Estelle shook her head. "I didn't see much after the voices started," she admitted. "I don't know what was happening. The doctors said I was getting better when we came here. And then he asked me to help him and put me in this thing. He said it would help him and I did whatever he asked because I wanted him to like me better. But then there were just voices. One of them made me do stuff. It wasn't like us. It was like I was part of one of Will's programs. And then he started adding in more voices and they were in so much pain..."

Estelle covered her ears and shook her head, but the screams were already echoing around them. Indira waved them away and quieted the area once more. It looked like it helped Estelle at least, who relaxed as they faded away and didn't try to bring them back. This place was acting as a second home to her for now, reflecting perhaps a little too much. Powerful though she was, she hadn't learned nearly enough while she was properly alive to know how to keep herself in check.

"So that's what he's trying to do to me," Indira said. "You know your brother has me captured now."

Estelle bristled, her sweet and vulnerable demeanor melting away, and she turned on Indira. "Good!" she snapped. "You banished me in here! You made me go away and it took so long to get back together! And you won't let me even try to save myself, so I'm *glad* he found you and he's going to make you like me! Maybe if he does, he'll let me go and he can just take you and make you do it instead."

For all her anger and vitriol, she really was just a kid. She didn't know what she was doing and, as much as Indira wanted to be, she couldn't be mad at her for the irrational actions of a child in her situation. Indira let out a calming breath, hating these moments that she had to be an adult. "So you're saying you want to go back?" she asked. She looked to the side and pressed on the walls to Estelle's prison. "If you're really sure, you could just go back to your body and those screams. Maybe by the time you get back, you'll already be out and they'll have put me in instead."

Estelle only managed to hold firm for a few seconds before she sealed up the walls of this place tight and changed the world around them to the much happier scene of people playing in a park in the middle of an intact metropolis. "No!" she said. "I don't want to go back to that. Please don't make me go back!"

"But you might not be in there anymore," Indira told her. "You might already be free."

"He'll never let me go," she said. Her voice was quiet and she didn't meet Indira's eyes. "I know he won't. Please. I don't want to go back there. They're already trying to bring me back, but I don't want to."

"Okay. But you're going to have to make it up to me somehow. Because now I'm going to be stuck doing what you do unless we work fast and you manage to help us take your brother down. They're going to realize I'm not actually in my body and I don't want them to get mad and take it out on my family. And… can they can use you to do that? Can they make you bring me back?"

Estelle looked guilty at the accusation. "You're going to do it?" she asked. "You're going to make him let me go and make him stop making me hurt people? I thought you said it was a stupid idea and that it was going to get Kyle killed."

"That's because your idea *is* stupid," Indira told her. "*My* idea has a lot of people who are putting themselves at risk because they already know what they're getting into and doing it because they want to. And who know what is happening and know to be careful. There's a big difference. But you need to do something to help us do it. You want to help us get you out of there for good, right?"

Estelle nodded and Indira could feel herself relax. She sat down on the grass, inviting Estelle to join her. "Has anyone ever taught you to do anything?" Indira asked leaning forward and blocking out the rest of the world except for the two of them. Estelle shook her head and eliminated the rest of the setting around them, staring enamoured into Indira's eyes as she tried to figure out what she was getting at. "You're a very powerful young woman," Indira continued, "but you're a little fractured right now. You should actually be able to do a lot more than you are currently doing, but I'm thinking it's because you've never had a lot of training or help."

"No one ever taught me anything," Estelle said, self-conscious. "They locked up my powers when I was little and then I didn't know what I was doing with them. And Will was so scared of them that he wouldn't talk to me and refused to even look at me when we were together. He hated me for them, so I just kept trying to hide them. Until I was useful…"

"It's okay," Indira said soothingly, trying to keep her from an emotional outburst right now. She needed to keep her calm. At the very least, she needed to stay calm enough to focus and try to do the things that Indira knew she should be able to do. "There's a little trick I learned a while ago that has to do with your projection. You remember back a while back when we were down underground and you drew me all the way in when I was only projecting a little bit of myself in there?"

Estelle thought back. "It's muddy," she said, thinking about it hard, but the memory of it slowly coming back to her. Indira tried to help along, giving an impression of the day around her to help until the memory finally caught. Estelle only remembered it as a vague thing, but it was an action she had taken on her own because she was curious. It was the start of her fascination with Indira. "I think I remember. I heard it in the screams."

As disturbing as that was, Indira managed to press forward with it. "Okay, I'm going to teach you to do that in reverse," she said. "If you can pull all of yourself in here, then there's not going to be anything left to keep all those people there. Without you, everything falls apart."

She hesitated. "Will is going to hate me if I do this."

"Estelle, you've already done everything he's asked. You enslaved all of Whitten for him and he still doesn't love you. Now concentrate. If you can get this, you're going to be able to save the city."

"You promise?" she asked.

Indira smiled at her. Good, she was on board. Indira got to work teaching her to pull herself away. It was an old trick that Estelle had clearly already learned to do in part already. It didn't take Estelle long to learn how to do the rest, to push past her fear of never being able to return until there was nothing left of her with her body. Indira hoped that this worked. She needed it to work. She didn't have any other ideas.

CHAPTER 21

CHARGE

THOUGH INDIRA HAD no idea where she was, Estelle was able to direct her back to Whitten once they were done. Estelle had pulled most of herself into her cocoon already and Indira was anxious to find out if anyone was still safe. She didn't even know how long she had been gone for or if any of them were still around.

Whitten was different when she looked at it, and it wasn't just that night had fallen while she was away. At first she wasn't sure what it was, but someone appeared to be trying to set the outer ring of it on fire. Confusion echoed through the outer circles of town. People still tried to figure out why they were remembering people that they had not seen in years, but now there was deep concern and panic as they realized the number of people who had gone missing. Others were starting to remember watching as people died in front of them, only to be forgotten a day later.

Peppering it all were those who were very determined to destroy in the name of freedom.

The closer to the center of town Indira looked, the calmer it was. No one seemed to notice the smoke filling the air. Their thoughts were a jumble of mundanity about the day and the sparse few who were worried for whatever their day or week brought them. There were flickers of clarity that something was happening, but those were fleeting and soon settled as the people fell into their nightly routines.

The police were a strange exception. Each and every one of them fought something happening in their heads. They didn't know what was happening to them, both finding that they had strange recollections of things they had done and had thought they saw at times, but they weren't sure if any of those things were real or not. Nothing felt real, but they still remembered it.

Either the effects of Estelle's absence from herself were more immediate than Indira assumed or Indira had been gone a very long time. The police were only suffering in moments and waves, but it was enough that she could tell something was working. The walls were starting to come down. She had to hope those things at the edges of town were people taking down the towers. She could really use the cavalry right now.

Indira focused on finding Matt first, glad to know that he was still thinking out there somewhere. The problem was where that somewhere happened to be, and she cursed herself for not erasing the location from his mind when she had the chance. He was already underground and he wasn't alone.

Indira hauled herself there and gave herself a physical projection. She would feel a lot better if she could feel like she was yelling at him in person. "What the hell are you doing here?" Indira demanded, looking between him and Esther. Brittany and Laura didn't stop and kept pressing forward, splitting off from the two of them. They were going to get themselves killed like this. It didn't exactly go well the last time and she wasn't going to let that happen again, even if it means knocking them all out right here. "I thought you were calling in the professionals."

"I did," Esther said, walking through her. Indira stayed with them, drifting alongside them. "They're taking down the towers. Big old distraction. That means we can save our own while the majority of their forces are distracted." She punctuated the words with kicking the door open.

"That door doesn't even have a lock on it," Indira said.

"And now we're in. So are you going to help us save you or not?"

"I'm sorry." Indira shook her head and started to push into their heads, telling them to turn back around and go sleep in the car until this was all over. It wasn't safe for them here and she wasn't going to have their deaths on her hands just because help was here and Indira's plan was in motion. As soon as Estelle managed to bring the rest of herself into her bubble in the sky, everything should collapse on its own. They didn't *need* to do this. She had to stop them.

Except that she couldn't. There was something stopping her from doing it. The more she pressed, the more backs of her hands tingled despite not having a physical presence. She looked down at them, then accusingly at Matt.

"I told you," Matt said with a bit of a smile as she fell in step beside him. "You aren't stopping me. And I'm not letting you stop anyone else. Now, are you going to help us?"

Indira wasn't happy about it, but at the very least she could keep them connected. She had to make sure they weren't getting themselves killed because they were stepping over one another. "You guys don't even have a plan!" she snapped at them, making sure they could all hear her. Matt exposed all the passages for them, but seeing what was coming didn't help last time. "It's not too late to turn back. Come up with a plan. *Let the professionals deal with it.*"

"It's fine, Damien's bringing them," Brittany told her. "He's just off getting that lock disabled and he and Alan will meet us here with whatever big guns he can find."

"You think they're going to disable his lock?" Indira asked. "Wait, if they're already coming, why are you here? You don't have to do this."

"Except one of the plans was to torch the place and everyone in it," Esther said. "They didn't decide yet. Damien and Alan are going to try to talk them out of it but... We don't want to risk it."

She knew she should argue, but Indira held her tongue. She wanted them safe and out of here, but there were a lot of people in here that would die if they went ahead with that plan. Penny was in there still, along with Uncle Ness and countless other friends and family that had been lost to Whitten over the years. If there was no guarantee to keep them from torching the place, then she could understand them wanting to at least try to save them.

Indira didn't want to be dead either. For now, she moved ahead of them, taking a better look at what was going on. The white room felt much further away today. It radiated the glow so softly, and had none of the pull that it used to. Estelle was likely gone now, she reminded herself, and the power that radiated from the room was from the rest who still remained in there. She wondered how long the effects would remain with Estelle gone; if they would wake up soon and break free on their own.

Not that it was the most important thing for them to worry about right now. "Rooms on the east still have a few zombies left," Indira told them, looking for anyone they hadn't thrown out to deal with what was happening on the outskirts of town. Best to take them out before they went to join the others, or they decided to wake up and ambush them. Those that were awake we all gathering in one place. "Most of them look like they're being put to use on the line to protect the room. I think I can get closer."

They rounded the corner and saw just how many people lined the halls outside the door to the white room. The hazmat suits did not move from their spot despite the chaos, not flinching at the loud bangs and yells coming from the east corridors. Laura and

Brittany went through the walls to join Ronnie in taking care of the remaining rooms.

Esther flicked a knife into her hand, adjusting the grip as she started to count them. "*You* are waiting for backup," Esther said. "If anything happens again, I'm going to need help bringing these guys back from whatever the hell that room does to them when they look at it so they don't die here."

"And you don't."

"I can."

The building rocked around them as Brittany and Laura collapsed the rooms and halls on the east side, bringing the parking lot and cars above them crashing down into the rooms to take them out. The hazmat suits didn't react to the chaos or to Esther charging at them until she landed her first blow. Laura and Brittany came swooping back with Ronnie and several small metal demons at their beck and call, all of them diving at the hazmat suits standing in their way.

Indira moved between them all, trying to decide which of the suits was dangerous and needed their powers suppressed, only to find that most of them were not very efficient in close quarters. Many were more prone to setting themselves on fire and continued to fight. Matt brought the rain down from the ceiling and doused the flames before they spread too far.

"Specks are turning on!" Indira called to them as she saw the red lights start to flicker into existence. Brittany and Laura

demanded to know where they were and Indira mentally highlight-
ed them, flicking their attention to each of them as they turned on
and switched modes. They were much slower to switch and Indira
hoped that meant they had time.

Small metal demons crawled up the walls, gnawing at each of
the specks. The lasers still cut through them, but there were many
more demons to take over. When one fell, another would take its
place until they got rid of every one of the specks.

Indira felt a pulse and it got much more difficult to move. She
saw that the powers around them stopped as Laura got punched in
the face and knocked back. Brittany didn't fare much better, nor did
anyone else. Esther was the only one up still, jumping out of the
way and retreating back a hallway, abandoning them as the rest of
them were taken down one by one.

"The hell was that?" Esther demanded. She shook her head,
but she kept her jaw locked as she looked back around the corner.
Everyone else was taken down to their knees and detained in a
row. Esther saw her father coming to meet them, an all too familiar
gun in hand and looking entirely too pleased with himself. "Hurry,
Indira, what do I need to do to get them out of there before my dad
starts shooting them?"

"Three of them take out powers," Indira said. "How quick
are you?"

"Quick enough," Esther said. "I'll take them down. You see
what you can do about reversing the brainwashing on my father
and we might just be able to keep them down."

Indira mentally pointed the suits out and Esther went to work. She worked a lot faster than anticipated, her knife moving through the suits and getting them each in the throat.

While she went to work, Indira went to Officer Nava. His mind was covered in the white sticky stuff, much like Matt's mind had been before. She had the uncomfortable realization that, while the influence over some minds was being pulled back as Estelle drew herself away, there was still the lingering effect from anyone who had been exposed to it for a long time. And Officer Nava had been here so long that the white had built up and rooted itself deep.

She began to pull on the white sheet that had burrowed so deeply in his head, like a weed with roots that had buried themselves far too deep in concrete. It stuck to her as she pulled it out, but there was nothing now to keep it there. It was still sticky and lingered, but it no longer held fast as she pulled away more and more.

Finally, the smile on his face faltered and he stumbled forward as he tried to understand what was happening. He stared at Indira, confusion replacing the smugness. It would be good enough, Indira decided, and she needed to get back to the fight.

"I did what I could," Indira told Esther, who was busy taking out one of the men holding Brittany. Brittany had her demons still working on the small specks that watched them, the demons taking any stray shot cast into the crowd. She let out a curse and a new one grew out of the wall to replace the fallen.

Down the hall, Officer Nava started barking orders, demanding that they take those kids down by any force necessary. Indira panicked, wondering if she hadn't actually gotten everything out of his head, but Esther didn't seem too concerned about it. She saw him hesitate at the sight of his daughter. He said her name, confusion flooding through him before he went back to insisting that they take down all the powers by any means necessary.

Matt was the last to free himself, though that looked like it was by choice. Something grew out from the ground around him and he used the wall as a hand to grab one of the hazmat suits and hold him in place. He wove the vines up to push more of them to the ceiling, trapping them. Esther came by him and passed him a knife, Matt not sure what she wanted him to do with it. "I'm not going to—"

"I need it enchanted," she said. "You can do that, right?"

"Encha— to do what?" he demanded.

"Just enchant it!" she snapped at him. Another hazmat suit went down in front of her. "You can do that, right?"

"Enchant it *to do what?*" he demanded. "There's *a lot* you can enchant something to do!"

Esther scrambled for the words, mentally flailing where her body was smooth and moved very deliberately. "I don't know! It needs to just do... *things!*"

"Just think it really loudly," Indira snapped her. "It will get passed along."

Matt frowned for a long moment before he looked down at the dagger, his hands already starting to work. "*Disenchant*," he told her. "You were looking for disenchant."

Indira wanted to ask why, but the answer was easy enough to glean off the top of her head. Though Indira had gotten rid of the psychic control, there was likely still magic at work to keep him obedient. Indira frowned at that, realizing what else that meant. That was why the white stuff was so sticky. It was a mix of psychic energy and magic.

Esther took up a position to keep everything off of him. With Laura and Ronnie back in the fight, the chaos returned. There were too many bodies working together in too small of a corridor. The space never stayed clear for long as more hazmat suits kept filing in, but Indira could see the last of them.

And so could Officer Nava, it seemed, as he raised the gun like it was the only thing that made sense to him anymore.

Matt passed the knife back to Esther and went back to the vines, catching anything that looked like too much of a problem and trapping them against the wall or ceiling. Indira worked with him to point out where the most dangerous ones were. She focused on everything happening, on all the people and trying to watch everyone's backs, but it all moved so quickly that Indira was starting to get dizzy and very tired.

"Kill them a—"

Esther dropped from her vantage point, hanging from the vines, and threw the knife over the crowd at her father. It landed hard in his shoulder and he dropped. Esther didn't stop moving, didn't even wait to see if her father was alright, before diving back into the fray.

There were no more waves of suits coming for them, and they were getting very good at keeping the hazmat suits from getting up again. They were able to take down what was left and soon they were finally through the swarm, leaving them with only corpses.

Breathing deep, they looked around, waiting for something else to come. Indira didn't know what else to do but look around and make sure that they were safe and done. The call center had been evacuated in the commotion and there were no more men left to don a hazmat suit and come after them remaining. Indira let herself materialize in the hall to talk to them as they caught their breath. "We're good," she said. "You're dad's still alive, though, Esther. What do you... Esther?"

Esther was slumped against the wall, but she wasn't thinking anymore. Her mind grew very quiet until she finally flickered out. Brittany and Laura went to her side, trying to nudge her awake and failing miserably at it. Indira knew why. She wasn't alive anymore, having gotten hit a little too badly at some point and she had kept going until she finally went down. Of all the things, Indira knew that this would happen to someone. She hoped it wouldn't be her again.

Yelling echoed in her ears from somewhere not too far away. Her body was around here somewhere, listening to someone on a tirade. She could hear something stirring by her body and they needed to move fast, but they were already close. They might actually be able to save her.

"She's gone," Indira said. "But she might be back. Grab her on the way out. You two, keep her safe until she wakes up again. She did it once before and it was a lot worse than this. She'll probably do it again. Matt, you make sure Officer Nava doesn't get back up for a while. I don't know what she did, but I'm thinking after seeing her aim, she wasn't trying to kill him."

"I got it," Matt said, stepping in. A dome appeared over Esther and she vanished under it. "She's just at my place," he told them. "She'll be safe until we get out of here."

A pang of guilt struck Indira even as she knew her body was being moved. They should be running. She wanted to be saved, but not at the cost of all of them. "Last chance to get the hell out of here before anyone else dies," Indira told them. She hoped that at least one of them would, but Esther's death had only made them more determined.

"No one else dies," Laura said. "You aren't getting rid of us. Now let's burn this place to the ground."

CHAPTER 22

THE WHITE ROOM

MATT LINGERED BACK with Indira, ready to grab someone as soon as the effects of the white room overtook them for
getting too close. Even Brittany and Laura were hesitant, seeing
how distrustfully Matt eyed the door, letting Ronnie step forward
to take the lead.

"Come on," he said. He was still tired, but ready for another
round. "They're in here, right? We just need to get everyone out."

The door resisted at first, but Ronnie was more than capable.
He yanked on the door and pulled it out by the hinges, eyes going
wide and cheeks flushing at the show of strength. Sheepishly he put
it down by the door and led the way in, the rest hesitating before
following.

Indira waited until she was sure no one was going to come
running out before she finally went in. It still felt very dangerous,
though less so than ever before. She almost didn't want to know
what was behind those doors, where she had abandoned Penny to

and where she may be getting placed right now. Part of her was still expecting to be pulled in and held there. There was no tug this time, and if her body was already in there, then she should go.

She stopped just inside behind the rest of them, looking around and taking it in. The whole room hummed with power, a reflection of those kept inside of it. She could see the web connecting them together as a white cloud, psychic static made heavy with magic and lingering in the air over everything. In the right hands it could be used to create whatever someone want, maybe even a whole universe, but now it didn't even move.

Visually, the room was massive; larger than it should have been, though oddly sterile. The lights were unnaturally bright, though that might have just been the sterile white of everything but those pods. Rows of pods lined the room like a field of corn, straight lines with glass windows to show which ones were occupied by humans. The faces in the pods stared out, eyes wide as their bodies were frozen, watching all and seeing nothing.

Wires and tubes ran neatly along the floor, marking walkways that all led back to a large device in the center. She could see the tube Esther had mentioned before, empty now though it was easily the size of an old comatose woman if it needed to hold one. Without her, there was a lingering energy that kept everything together, more than Indira was expecting.

"Can you feel that?" Laura asked, looking around. Indira knew Laura wasn't seeing the same thing as she was, but she could feel the lingering cloud of power. They all could.

"Take down that middle thing," Indira told them. "Once it's gone, they're screwed and they can't keep this going. I think. Get as many people out of here as you can. Leave as soon as you think everything is too hot. Keep Matt alive so he can pop you all out of here if everything goes to shit."

"And what the hell are you doing?" Matt demanded. He reached for her, but his hand passed through her. "It sounds an awful lot like you're ditching us."

"I can hear my body around here somewhere," Indira told her. "And Chief Hollins has a very interesting plan to raise everyone in this room to murder a lot of people. And unlike the people outside, everyone in here is actually still alive and conscious and is going to know full well what they are doing and have no way of stopping themselves. Unless you think Penny's going to enjoy being made to murder a bunch of people coming to save her, including her brother, I think you'd do best to let me head off."

He relented, though he wasn't happy about it. Indira wanted to do something to comfort him, already feeling her hand start to itch, but nothing came to her. "Just get them free and get out of here before someone torches the place," she said. "If you could, find Quantum and punch him in the face for me. He really deserves it after all the crap he's put me through."

Indira faded away as she heard the first crash as they got to work. Part of her hoped that they would work quickly and have time to come find her body, but there were so many pods and so many people they needed to get out first. Maybe no one would come to torch the place in the end. Maybe there would be time to save her too.

Her body was easy to find now that she was close. Chief Hollins was yelling and she was fairly certain her body was in a considerable amount of pain right now. She had no intention of going into it just yet but, as she drew closer, she found herself being pulled faster and faster along to the place where her body was inevitably kept. Physically, it wasn't very far. There was a small room just above where they were now, a place that didn't feel like it should exist despite how close she got to it.

The closer she came, the more she could feel something trying to pull her in. Indira didn't let it jerk her any more quickly, maintaining a very even pace until she got into the room and stopping just on the other side of the wall. She could see herself lying on a table, unconscious as she had left herself, with several things applied to her head. They'd cut off her hair in order to connect her to some device sitting next to her on the table, plugged into Chief Hollins' computer.

She tried her best not to react to what she was seeing, but she couldn't help but feel a pang of anger and depression as she saw herself with short hair. It was a stupid thing to latch onto, but she hadn't been expecting it and she just looked *wrong* with her hair that short.

"Only a matter of time," Chief Hollins said, drumming his fingers on the table as he turned up the intensity on whatever his device was. Indira felt something jolt in her to pull her in, but she kept from getting any closer to her body. She clung as best she could to the wall and saw her father in the corner, being suspended in the air and with his face pressed into a crack in the drywall. The rest of his body hung limp. Uncle Ness was there, not moving as he watched her father.

Sitting next to Indira on the table was Aunt Tess, now in a wheelchair with her head completely devoid of any activity. Chief Hollins had given up on her, leaving her there after realizing that she was unable to help him in his plans any longer. Now, his plan was to use whatever was on his computer to make Indira return.

A shot rang out below them, followed by another and another. Indira wanted to look, to make sure they were okay and to see what they were up against, but couldn't leave. The only direction she could move was closer to her body, and she would be of no use to anyone there. He'd have her and her powers if she got too close.

Something flickered on the screen and he looked around, laughing. "I know you're here, Indira," Chief Hollins said. "You can't run from me that easy. I already have your uncle and your father. If you want them both back and alive, you should hold up your end of the bargain. Your friends won't survive down there, and you know I have nothing left to lose by making these two suffer."

Indira almost didn't hear the pounding on the door through the sound of gunfire below. "Dad?" Kyle called from the other side. What the hell was he doing here? Estelle's influence must have still been on him, drawing him here to try and do something that was going to get him killed. Indira couldn't stop him now.

Kyle kicked at the door, making it rattle on its hinges. "Dad, let me in! What are you doing in there? It's chaos out here and your cops are *shooting* people all over the place! You have to stop them! There's stuff that's just shooting randomly from the walls in here! I don't know what's happening, but you have to stop it!"

He kicked the door again and this time it popped open. Chief Hollins was not perturbed by the new witness to what he was doing.

Kyle had no idea what he was looking at. There was a young woman lying on the table with things sticking out of her head. There were people in the corner that were unconscious and partially through a wall. One of them was floating. He couldn't put anything together, not even that it was Indira on the table. It wasn't her hair, and his father was doing…

"Dad!" he demanded, standing at the door with terror flooding his face. "What is all of this?"

"Necessary," Chief Hollins said calmly, turning up the settings on his computer. Indira felt the pull back to her body grow stronger. "This is what we need to do to keep the peace in here."

There was hostility building up in Kyle, Indira could feel it, and he was going to do something drastic. And if he did, he was going to get killed. No more people should die from this. "You can't do this," he said, playing the hero role just as well as Indira knew he would. "You can't just *do this* to people. Dad, you have to stop whatever this is. Is that Aunt Tess? What are you—"

As soon as the gun came out, Indira acted. She had already seen enough people dead from this and she knew Kyle wasn't going to bounce back from it as easily as Esther was. He'd be like all the others that she never saw again. She leapt at Chief Hollins, feeling the pull back to her body get unbearably strong as she got close. Working with pure desperation, she grabbed Chief Hollins out of his body and dragged him up out of reality and into the collective subconscious.

It took too long before she finally felt like she couldn't hear her body trying to drag her back anymore. She kept running into the chaos, needing to get farther away. She didn't stop until she couldn't hear anything anymore, choosing this place for her final stand. Indira created a place around them and threw Chief Hollins to the side. His figure fell limply and crumpled to the ground. He was not used to the idea of not having a body. Indira tried to catch her breath. She was exhausted already from having run so far, but she was far from done.

She created some space between them, hand on the back of her head and cracking her neck. Just a little more to do. She let out a slow breath as she turned to the approaching Chief Hollins. She waved her hand, raising him up in the air and stopping his movements as she got closer to him. He dangled in the air, glaring daggers at her and struggling to get down to no avail.

"Stop that," Indira said, lowering him back down to the ground, but still keeping him from moving any closer to her. She shrank him so that he stood a foot shorter, which only seemed to make him angrier. "You're done, Chief Hollins. Will Hollins. You don't have anything left to do."

He growled and spat at her. She didn't let the liquid land on her, instead sending it right back into his face. He did not much like that, but there was nothing he could do about it. He snarled and glared at her. "*I made peace,*" he told her. "I kept the place from being destroyed by your kind."

Indira shook her head. "You murdered *my kind.* You turned my kind into zombies and set them on the ones who were still alive. And you turned the ones that you could use into batteries so that you could force your sister into the thing that kept this whole place running."

"Shame she had an expiration date," he said. "Five years I got this place running. And if you think you're going to stop me from making you do the same thing, girl, you are sorely mistaken. What do you think is going to happen here? You think you'll be able to resist the call forever? Eventually you're going to have to go back in there. Once you do, you think I'm going to just let your uncle and your father go? You really think you can live with yourself knowing you could have saved my sister from her evil brother by taking her place?"

Indira threw him back and let him move on his own again. He fell to the ground, landing hard on the nothing that was around them and he got to his feet. "And where do you think you're going?" Indira asked. "Even if I get pulled back in there, what do you think is happening to you? Can you find your way back?"

"Once you're back, then—"

"No," Indira said. "If I don't bring you back and put you back, you don't go back. You'll be stuck here forever. And I'm not seeing a lot of reasons to bring you back. You've done a lot of bad things, Hollins. I don't see any reason at all that I should ever let you return. I think Whitten's going to be a much better place without you."

"Then how are you planning to get your uncle back?" he asked. "You forget, I'm in control of my sister and my sister currently has your uncle under my control. And if I ask her nice, I can make your uncle kill your father. And he'll believe he did it of his own free will. You know what happens to heroes who do that?"

Indira shook her head. She wasn't about to let herself be intimidated in a place she made herself. She let the city rise up around her, which unsettled Chief Hollins, but she didn't let herself feel even a little bad about her actions. Instead, she watched as he grew uncomfortable about the city that he had come to take care of so fiercely over the years and how it towered over him, watching him and wanting him to stare back into it.

"Do you know what you've done to the people of Whitten?" she asked. "You've made it a little hell that has killed so many people. We've learned to watch what we say. You said powers were legal so long as there was no heroism or villainy, but that's not true at all, is it, Chief Hollins? Instead, you were listening. Always listening. You shot my brother for saying some words and wanting the freedom to speak. You always listened and never let us have a moment's peace. And so guess what I'm going to do."

The specks appeared around the city. They were all red, all listening carefully, waiting for the next words that would trigger them. He was not scared and didn't even look at them. He hadn't learned to fear those little red eyes watching him yet, but he was going to learn. Indira was going to make sure he learned how much she put her and everyone else through with their constant surveillance.

"It was necessary," Chief Hollins said. "I kept my city safe."

No sooner did he get the words out than he felt a sharp shot go through his shoulder. He cried out in pain, stunned that he felt it so clearly as he fell forward. He grasped the shoulder, looking back at the city in betrayal as his hand came away bloody. He looked back at her, a cruel smile on his face and a laugh on his lips. "You think this will make me change my mind?"

"It's not good to lie, Chief Hollins," Indira said, putting on her good girlfriend voice. "I won't take you back if you keep lying."

"I won't let your father live if you— *Argh!*" he cried as another one went through his side.

"You could try running away from them," Indira suggested, her voice sounding as interested in his plight as a customer service representative. "Now that you know where they are. Or you could just stop lying and threatening people. Stop trying to make us go away because you don't like us. You know how to do that, right Chief Hollins? You can have those opinions all you want, but you just aren't allowed to talk about them or act on them anymore. It's fair, right?"

Chief Hollins looked at her with eyes that wanted to kill her, but he didn't dare say anything. Instead he got up and started moving as he continued to think terrible, awful things in his mind. Indira let his thoughts echo out loud around him. He wasn't going to be able to get away from the punishment that was this Whitten that easily. She wouldn't let him. And he was never getting out of here.

"I'll make you get in that damn machine." His thoughts echoed loudly around him. The specks lit up and opened fire. She let some of them miss as he kept trying to move and dodge them, though others clipped him still as he tried to get away. *"This is just the kind of thing I'd expect of powers like you. You're all alike and you think you can just get away with anything. I'm levelling the playing field."*

Indira followed him as he tried to run and get away, but Whitten kept following him. On a bright, clear, sunny day, there were even people around who ignored his pain. She kept letting him go, running away from the specks and their laser eyes as his thoughts broadcasted so loudly around him. He was falling very quickly to despair and Indira was enjoying his pain. Perhaps a little too much.

It felt like she was justified in having a little of this. He'd put them all through so much pain and torment. He had her lying unconscious on a table after kidnapping her, cut off her hair while she was out cold, and tried to force her back into her body so that she could spend the rest of her days forcefully enslaving the people of Whitten to maintain this powers ban. This was no more than he deserved and she was not about to let it stop just because she worried she might feel uncomfortable about it later.

Besides, they might be torching the whole place soon with them still in it. His suffering might not even last for long.

"I'll let your father live!" he offered at last. He was running as fast as he could as Whitten started to close in on him. As he felt more claustrophobic, as the pain he felt got worse, as his attempts to run were getting harder, he was finally starting to relent. And as he relented, he tried to change tactics.

"I'll kill them all as soon as I get out of here."

"It doesn't sound like you're letting anyone live," Indira told him, a shot going straight through his back. Chief Hollins fell on the ground face first and Indira knelt by him. She kept her eyes wide and full of that innocence that she maintained when she was with her boyfriend's parents. She looked down at him, curious.

"You were going to shoot your own son," she reminded him. "You had your finger on the trigger. I wonder what you would have done to him if he was like us. If he was like your sister, I guess everything would have been perfect. He could have replaced Estelle. You wouldn't have had to deal with me."

"Bitch," he coughed, the blood from his mouth landing on the ground. "You can't kill me in here. This is just in my head, right? You can't kill me in my own head. I'll still be alive and one day, you'll feel so bad, like all you heroes do, and you'll come back. One day, you'll let me out. And when you do—"

A shot went through his throat, silencing him. He wasn't unconscious. He would never be unconscious. But for the moment, he couldn't move and he couldn't speak. She thought that was enough for the moment and ceased the attack on him, at least long enough to have a few last words with him before she let herself out.

"I think you mistake me for a hero, Chief Hollins," Indira told him. "I never wanted any of that. I didn't even use my powers before I came here very much. I wanted nothing to do with any of the hero stuff, but then here you come along and you make it all my problem. So really, Chief Hollins, *you* made me. You made the powered hero that eventually took you down and freed the other heroes of Whitten from your fear and tyranny. Villains too, I guess."

Indira let out a sigh. "But I'm no hero. I'm not going to feel remotely bad about leaving you here to rot. And you are never getting back to torment the city or your sister or your son again. And no, my uncle won't be happy that I did it. Wrong hand to try playing now, Hollins. You've destroyed too many lives. And for that, you don't get to go back."

She patted him lightly on the head and turned on his thoughts and the specks once more. "You enjoy the Whitten I made for you. Remember, no more lying and no more trying to silence the powers. You won't be hurt forever. The specks will never kill you like they killed so many of us. And you'll heal so you can just keep getting shot over and over again for all eternity. Think of it like a superpower. I took the idea from you, so I hope you really enjoy being able to run for the rest of your days. Until someone comes along and finally pulls the plug on your body."

With that, Indira turned around, leaving Chief Hollins to his Whitten. He would never break out and, as she kicked the little contained universe further out into the nothingness, she knew that no one would ever find him again.

Chapter 23

FLOATING

INDIRA SUPPOSED IT was a good thing that she wasn't dead yet. It felt like she'd been here a week, aimlessly drifting through nothing, which meant that they probably hadn't torched the place. Or, at least, they managed to get her out of there before they did.

She wondered sometimes if her friends were alive, but those thoughts were quickly pushed aside. It didn't really matter whether they were or not if she was stuck out here. She didn't know where she was, never having seen anywhere that looked so sparse. There was no chaos, no hectic jumble of thoughts to look through to let her know what might have happened or how long she had been gone. She hadn't noticed when she ran out here, but it seemed she was out too far for anything but herself and her own thoughts.

Sometimes Indira would make herself little places to make up for the lack of having even another mind around here to walk into, just to give herself something to do. She thought she might run into other people up here eventually, but there was just a lot of nothing everywhere. There weren't colours or shapes or anything at all. It was all empty.

Indira made herself modes of transportation every now and then to entertain herself as she traveled through the nothing, not sure where she was going to end up. Her mind often drifted and she would surprise herself with a fish or a creature of some sort to keep her company and to talk to now and then, but she was getting comfortable with the fact that she might never find her way back, doomed to wander until her body gave out.

It wasn't an easy conclusion to come to. Normally, though, she would never be gone for this long. She had never been this far out, though, and she was too turned around to be able to find her way back to her body. As much as she never wanted this to happen, she had made a mistake and she had plenty of time now to accept that. Lots of mistakes. She was fine with her fate and, for the moment, hoped that one day someone might be able to come out this far so she'd have someone to talk to who wasn't just a figment of her imagination. Someone with news. Someone who had heard of Whitten.

She couldn't help sometimes thinking about what might have happened to Whitten since she left. She didn't want to think too much about the people, not wanting to accept that someone might have died amidst those gunshots. That they might have met ends fighting at the edge of the city or somewhere in the aftermath, whatever the aftermath of it all was.

Maybe everyone was off living normal lives after having moved out of the place by now. Maybe they evacuated the town and helped people resettle in other places while they dismantled the technology. Maybe the town just turned back into a normal budding metropolis. Maybe the whole place had been burning for years already and the flames would never go out.

She knew that wouldn't be the case, but without ever having to be there, she never had to know. There would be such a mess to clean up if they succeeded. There would be only bodies to remove if they failed. Either way, Whitten was going to have trouble getting back on its feet. The Speckled City that had banned heroes, that place was never going to be the same again. Even if they didn't evacuate the place, she wondered if anyone was going to return there after this mess.

She also wondered about her family. They would know to at least keep the radio on for her, but they didn't know that she was too lost to ever return. Indira was hopeful that they would give up after a little while. She would eventually start to lose her mind and unravel in this nothingness if she never found reality again, which was a distinct possibility. She really hoped they would pull the plug on her well before that, actually. Going mad from solitude and nothingness was not how she wanted to go.

Besides, if she woke up, she was going to have to deal with short hair. The more she thought about it, the more she hated it. It was hacked off and horribly uneven, not to mention that she had never had her hair that short. It was disconcerting. They just wanted to do it to stick her in that machine to transfer her consciousness into it. It couldn't have been necessary to cut her hair for it. How old was the machine they were using for it that they needed to do that? Not that it mattered out here, but it still bothered her.

Already she'd been left alone with her thoughts for too long. She didn't even know how long it had been, but she knew it was still far too long. She wanted to get back, if she was being honest, short hair and all. But she knew how unlikely it was that she was ever going to get out of here. She didn't even have a concept of time anymore. It could have been hours or years, she just didn't know.

When she saw something off in the distance, she thought nothing of it. She made herself a small oasis in the middle of the nothing, scattering the sky with stars and lying out on a blanket on a grassy green hill to watch them. She was busy wondering how much she could do with her life in here before they finally pulled the plug on her. The thing in the distance approached as a shooting star coming down to earth and she smiled, flicking at it and knocking it backwards to hit the other stars around it. Indira didn't expect it to talk.

"Hey!" the shooting star yelled at her, trajectory changing and zooming back down towards her. It became a person as it drew closer, and not a happy one at that. "Way to be ungrateful! Do you know how hard it's been to find you?"

Indira narrowed her eyes at the glimmer in the sky as it drew closer, realizing that she had imagined herself an Estelle. Except that this one wasn't just a figment of her imagination. The other girl appeared to actually be there and she was coming right for her. Estelle landed heavily on her feet next to her.

"Estelle?" Indira asked. She wasn't entirely convinced that this wasn't just a really convincing figment of her imagination. She had been fooled by a fridge flying at her across space a little while ago and dodged when it tried to offer her some food. That was an embarrassing and strange daydream that she was happy she would never have to explain, not even to another figment of her imagination. Maybe.

"You're not crazy," Estelle told her, offering her a hand up. It did feel like it was the real Estelle, albeit more complete than she had been before. Now she left an impression on Indira, who was able to feel the fatigue off of her, and the mild annoyance. "Not about me, anyway. But you are really far out. It took me forever to find you out here."

Indira took her hand, slowly working over in her mind what this meant. "I wasn't really expecting to be found. You know, ever. You're not here to trap me in a bubble and kick me out any farther, are you? Because I'm kind of already lost in space and that's not really going to be much of a change for me."

"I'm bringing you back," Estelle told her, hauling her forward and leading the way. Indira could feel them moving quickly through the darkness and let herself be led by the hand. The stars fell away and a world she didn't create started to appear around her. This didn't even feel that far. "You managed to help screw up a lot of stuff back in Whitten. It's the least I can do to thank you for that and for getting rid of my brother. I should thank you for that, I suppose."

"You've been back?" Indira asked, not wanting to think about how close she must have been to people all this time. "How's the place doing?"

"I don't know," Estelle said. "It's not like I thought it would be. They changed the law about the superheroes as soon as they found out about all the zombies and the people who were being used for the brainwashing and stuff, though. They weren't happy about all of that and the mayor came on and reversed it, but some people are saying that the papers aren't signed yet."

"That happens sometimes," Indira said. "Laws about heroes tend to take some work and litigation to get passed, even on the local level. Are the heroes still in town, though? Are they being kicked out or anything?"

Estelle shook her head. "The new Chief, he said that they need-ed all the help they could get right now. And since my brother's kind of comatose now, they're not going to try him for the stuff he's done. They're trying to figure out how much of what's happened was a result of the mind control he set up and how much was people doing things willingly. It's turning into such a big mess and no one really knows what's going on, but since so many people in Whitten are from hero areas, they are trying to help keep things in order and keep everything moving."

"Who's the new Chief? Is he any good?"

"Guy named Jericho Nava. Esther's father? And Esther came back, by the way," she added, knowing Indira's question before she asked it. "She woke up the next day after everything happened without a scratch on her. She's been worried about you. Everyone has. When they torched the place, everyone but you and me and my brother woke up."

"What happened to Kyle?"

"He got out fine. He was a bit shaken up about the whole thing, but I think he was more bothered by the fact that his dad was never going to face trial after finding out everything that he'd done. When it was safe, people started talking about the specks around the city and that's been the first thing everyone's been working on getting rid of. They aren't on anymore, but no one wants to risk this kind of thing happening again. Especially not now that they remember."

"Oh god, right," Indira said with a groan. "They're going to keep remembering now, aren't they?"

"It's kind of a mess out there," Estelle told her. "But you're still going back, even if you don't want to. There's a lot of people that want to ask you some stuff and everyone's been really worried because you haven't woken up yet. It's been a while. Apparently you've never been gone this long before."

"How long have I been gone for?" Indira asked. She was both curious and dreading the answer. "Has my hair grown back yet?"

"It's been about two months," Estelle told her, looking back at her like that was the worst question she could have possibly asked. "I'm not going to leave you out here until your hair grows back. You had a lot of hair."

Indira could see things she recognized again. There were people here, some dreaming while others were very awake and buzzing with thoughts and ideas. She made no move to try and discern what was actually going on. It didn't matter. After so long of floating in nothingness, this was what she had stopped hoping for. People and minds, thinking and dreaming all around her.

Stranger, she could hear something. Music. From her ears.

"I'm going to wake up again, aren't I?" she asked finally, almost bemused. "You came after me so that I could wake up again. I'm not going to just be stuck wandering through space forever." She smiled, though she couldn't help but feel apprehensive. Estelle warned her of the chaos that was waiting for her, but she was also going to get to see her body and her family again. Her friends might still even be there. Whichever ones were still alive.

"I'll see you around, Indira," Estelle told her. She went behind her and gave her a shove. Indira let herself fall back down to her body. "Go on. Wake up."

Chapter 24

REBUILDING

HER EARS FELT cloudy and her mouth like a desert, dry and gritty. The rest of her body came back slowly. She wasn't sure it was coming back at all at first. She thought she'd become one with the bed and she felt more than a little disgusting as her body greeted her with numbness, then tingling as her senses started to come back to her. It was strange not feeling the urge to throw up, but she doubted she could move that far. Everything felt like static and she almost wanted to leave it again.

The radio blared next to her and she was in her own bed at least, still in the same clothes from that day and placed under the sheets. She pried her eyes open to find her room was much the same as she had left it. She was already dizzy from the sunlight streaming in. It would be summer now, which would explain why she felt so disgusting. She was hot and sweating and suddenly wishing for telekinesis so she could turn on the air conditioning.

Slowly, Indira pushed herself up, her whole body slowly coming back to life after being in stasis for so long. She groaned and massaged the feeling back into her hands before she reached over and grabbed the water to help with her throat. As expected, her family of psychics were familiar with her needs and had water and a snack waiting for her by her bed in the event that she woke up. She was grateful for it and for not having a lot of people around her as soon as she woke. She needed a minute to adjust to what was happening and being alive again.

She didn't need the radio for that, though. Gingerly, she reached over, finding her limbs weak as she hit the button to turn it off. She was left with quiet and the sounds of the house.

In the next room, she heard shuffling and feet. Her door opened and she saw Shiraz standing there, one arm in a sling and looking at her with surprise, shock, and relief. She could tell that he never thought she was going to wake up again. Seeing her sitting up and looking completely aware of her surroundings left him struggling to figure out just what to do next.

"Think quieter," Indira told him. Her voice was quiet and hoarse, but she pressed on. "Didn't you used to knock?"

"That was before you decided to be a corpse!" he countered, coming over to give her a hug and welcome her back to the living. "Don't do that again, Indi. We were worried you weren't going to come back."

"I didn't think I'd make it back either," she said, pulling back and smiling at him. "But don't tell anyone about it yet," she said quickly, knowing that he was thinking about it. "I am disgusting and I'm not having them come by here to see me looking like this. Ugh, and I haven't even seen what they did to my hair for myself yet."

"You look like a lesbian."

There was a click at the window as Indira looked, Esther now tapping on the screen of her phone before pocketing it. Indira knew that the photo had been sent out and it was too late to argue it now, not that she had the energy to. Esther bound out of the window to her bed, hesitating to embrace her and pulling herself back at the last moment.

"How many more people are breaking in here and seeing me like this?" she asked. She ran a hand through her hair, stopping as she realized how light it was. Right. It was short now. She snapped her hand back, glancing at the mirror. She couldn't see herself from here, and was almost glad for it.

"Mom and Dad aren't home and Uncle Ness went back to Vancouver," Shiraz told her. "I need to tell them you're awake."

Indira nodded and looked at Esther.

"About five minutes?" Esther said.

Indira let out a deep sigh. "I am so gross," she said.

"They'll still be happy to see you awake. I know I am."

"Who's still alive?"

"Everyone," Shiraz told her. "Although your boyfriend doesn't want anything to do with you anymore. Apparently you kind of mind melted his dad."

"We broke up before that, it's fine." Indira rubbed her face, her fingers trailing to her temples and pressing into them for a moment. There was a pounding, but it didn't seem to be coming from in her head. There were more minds in the house. "Everyone lived?" she asked.

"Indira!"

Indira didn't have a chance to even look before a pair of arms were thrown around her, knocking her back to the bed. Esther lurched forward to help Indira back up as Shiraz laughed and moved out of the way, taking his phone out of his pocket and going to the door to give her a moment.

It took Indira a few seconds to realize who had tackled her. "Penny?" she asked, almost not believing it. But she was real and she was here. Her brown eyes were full of life and showed no signs of the horrors that she must have experienced while she was gone. Matt was even standing behind her, nodding like he was confirming her suspicions. She put a hand on Penny's bare arm and she was even warm under her fingers, sweating in the heat of the room. "You're alive. You got out."

"And so did you!" Penny beamed. "You saved us Indira."

You're a hero. It wasn't said in those words, but Indira could hear it echoing in their thoughts. It warmed her in a way that confused her and left her speechless. She'd saved people, helped bring down the system that kept them living in fear, and they thought she might have died in the process. It did sound heroic but...

She'd let them think that if they wanted. For right now, she was happy to know that they were all alive and well. And she was less happy to know that both Shiraz and Esther had now messaged several more people about her far too late resurrection.

"If more people are showing up, I want a shower before I see them," she said, looking pointedly at the two on their phones. "Help me up."

ABOUT THE AUTHOR

TANYA LISLE IS a novelist from Metro Vancouver, British Columbia, who has series littered across genres from supernatural horror to young adult fantasy. She began writing in elementary school, when she started turning homework assignments into short stories and continued this trend well into university. While attending Simon Fraser University, she developed an appreciation for public domain crossovers and cross-platform narratives. She has a shelf full of notebooks with more story ideas than pens lost to the depths of her bag. Now she writes incessantly in hopes of finishing all of them.

Thankfully, her cat, Remy, has figured out how to shut off Tanya's computer when she needs to take a break.

www.ingramcontent.com/pod-product-compliance
Lightning Source LLC
Chambersburg PA
CBHW031211260626
47169CB00007B/2013